FIGHT after FLIGHT

A MILITARY ROMANCE

CLAIRE CAIN

Cover Design by Jess Mastorakos - Jess@jessmastorakos.com

E-Book ISBN: 978-1-954005-87-7

Print book ISBN: 978-1-954005-47-1

To the spouses and partners who love someone in the military. It is a beautiful, wild thing we're doing. It doesn't always feel so glamorous, but I hope you know I think you're amazing. Glad to be on this journey with you.

Dear reader,

Fight After Flight is a military romance about two distant friends falling in love while healing hurts. While it's generally lighthearted, it may contain content not suitable for some readers.

The heroine's brother is killed in action years prior to this book, and the heroine and hero both grapple with their grief and the ripple effect it has on their choices prior to the book.

I hope readers who find this content to be particularly sensitive can make the best decision for their health and happiness. I want you to walk away with only happy, lovely feelings, and I hope you'll feel safe proceeding with this information in mind. If you have questions or need more information, contact me at claire@clairecainwriter.com.

My very best to you,

Claire

NOTE FROM THE AUTHOR

This series focuses on soldiers stationed overseas. OCONUS is the military acronym that stands for Outside the Continental United States. So really, it's what military personnel say when they're stationed somewhere other than the 48 continental states.

Any posting in Germany is an OCONUS duty station.

This series was formerly titled the OCONUS Bonus Series, but since that's not very clear for civilian readership, we've got a fresh series title. I couldn't skip this little intro, though, because the OCONUS setting is such a big part of the series. Being a service member outside the US is unique!

I hope you'll enjoy a peek at my fictionalized version of being stationed in Germany, which is based on my time living in Bavaria as a military spouse—truly some of my favorite years so far.

CHAPTER ONE

Bec

Muffled voices hummed outside my office door. Each echo set the cadence to which my heart pounded, shooting adrenaline through me in rough, angry jolts that caused my hands to shake.

The handle on the door lowered. My breath evaporated —if that was a thing breath could do. Like it got robbed from my lungs. I couldn't catch it—it ran away like a coward. Not unlike me.

And there he was.

"Bec."

I blinked, the sound of his voice harsh and beautiful. Familiar and yet new. I stood.

"Thatcher."

His face—one I'd known to be typically smiling and kind and warm and wonderful, right up until the last few weeks before I'd left—looked older. His eyes, like his skin, were still deep brown, his gaze probing. The cut of his cheeks and jaw were masculine and appealing, his lips sculpted and, I knew, ever so soft. He still shaved his head like he had before, the dark curve of his skull serving to highlight his beautiful face all the more.

But today, notably, no welcoming crinkle feathered at the sides of his eyes, nor did those lips curve up into a smile. I couldn't see his perfect white teeth. I couldn't see much of the man I'd known.

His dark brows dipped low. "What are you doing here?"

I blinked again, temporarily frozen. "I work here."

He shook his head slightly, like he hadn't meant to say what he had. "I mean, what are you doing working *here* at Kugelfels? I thought you were in Belgium or something."

He'd thought of me? Had ideas about where I should be? Somehow, this only made me feel more wretched, especially after the way I had treated him. "I considered it. But then this position opened, and I wanted to come here because Emily Wender, the director, was my old boss at Fort Campbell."

The words *Fort Campbell* fell hard into the room. The air seemed to flatten out under their weight, and my breath, which had returned out of thin air, came out in a pant. My hands shook and I folded my arms across my chest, tucking them in tight for protection.

"It's..." he trailed off, then licked his lips. "It's good to see you, Bec."

I wanted to close my eyes against his words. Why was this hitting me so hard? Oh, God, it was.

"I... you too."

What else could I say? *I've dreamed about this*? Or, *I've dreaded and longed for this in equal measure*? Or better yet, *I missed you so much it hurt*?

I couldn't. I wouldn't.

The tightness in his posture relaxed a bit, his shoulders and neck less rigid now. "This is crazy. After all this time..."

His gaze roamed over my face, and some of that light, sweet quality he'd always had entered his expression. My stomach flipped, his eyes on me no less affecting than they'd ever been.

"Yeah," I scraped out.

He smiled. Just a closed-mouth smile, but it slapped at me, reminding me of too many things.

Memories of meeting him before he and Ben and my twin brother, Dillon, deployed. Memories of seeing him after—after Dillon had died and I became a venerated Gold Star Family member. The crashing, aching loss fisting my heart in a vise so unforgiving, I hadn't felt it so strongly in years.

"Well, listen, I know it's closing time. I just—I saw you and had to say hi. Let's grab coffee and catch up sometime."

Meet with him. Again? That required superhuman strength I did not possess. I crushed my teeth together, my jaw aching with the contact. When I spoke, it was breath and air more than sound, the effort to speak one I hadn't realized would be such a challenge. "I, uh..."

He tilted his head, his smile patient. "Why don't we exchange numbers and we can arrange it that way. I'm sure you've got to—"

"No."

The sound of my voice cut through the room, and my eyes widened at how cold it sounded. I needed him to leave, and I didn't want his number. I didn't want coffee with him. And how could he possibly want it with me?

His expressive face didn't hide his response. His brows

rose, and surprise, a flash of hurt, then frustration settled there.

"Okay..." he said, sounding confused.

"Sorry. I just... I can't."

His mouth opened, then shut, and his lips flattened into a grim line. "Okay then."

He left, and the door swung shut. I collapsed into my chair, spent from what had been mere minutes. But these had been minutes with Thatcher Wild, which gave the time a whole other—draining, intense—dimension I was not ready for.

I made it home without crying all over myself. Miraculously.

I'd had plans to get drinks with Emily, but I'd messaged her I wasn't feeling well, then slipped out of the building before she saw me. Fortunately, her office door had been closed, so I didn't have to work too hard to evade her.

My heart hammered all the way home. It was only a twenty-minute drive, but I couldn't calm down. I couldn't believe it was *him*.

I'd longed to see him. I'd thought about calling him, e-mailing... but he was inextricably wrapped in the feelings I'd left behind. The useless sadness, the absolute finality of my brother's life. Somehow, Ben had escaped that correlation, but Thatcher...

Ben Holder, Thatcher Wild, and my twin brother, Dillon Jones, had met at Fort Campbell as lieutenants six years ago. They'd become fast friends—best friends. And then my brother was killed in action during their year-long deployment to Afghanistan, and half my heart left this earth.

Everything changed for me in a moment. My mom called with the news and I changed. Forever.

Thatcher and I had e-mailed before we met in person. It sounded weird now, but long story short, we got close before we ever saw each other. And when we did, we kissed, spent as much time as we could during the few weeks before he, Ben, and Dillon deployed, and continued growing close during the deployment.

Until my ability to do anything other than avoid the chasm in my chest—the sucking, grasping reality of the death of my favorite person on Earth—took over. I had no room for anyone and no hope for a relationship with Thatcher. Especially because he functioned just fine. Ben nearly self-imploded upon his return months after Dillon's death, but Thatcher seemed... sturdy. Fine.

I never begrudged him that, though I didn't understand it. He'd grieved, I believed, and then he just kept on. And I couldn't face the reality that Dillon no longer shared this life with me.

It took nearly two years of plodding through the days and using any tactics I could to escape my reality before I had the guts and vision to make a change. In that haze of avoidance, I'd promised Ben and Thatcher, who'd taken on brotherly roles checking in on me, I wasn't going off the deep end, as Ben had once said. And then I'd left.

I'd been so afraid to leave the last place we'd spent time together. Dillon had only lived in the apartment we planned to share for a few weeks before he deployed, but it had been enough to make me terrified of leaving. Of losing the last *place* I had with him.

Eventually, I'd realized I had to go. I had no way to keep

on functioning there. I stayed strong and focused on work, occupied myself with other people like my friend Erin, and just... gritted through the weighty grief. I didn't quite block it out, but I didn't allow it to settle in and help me process the loss. Like a wound that needed air and light, exposure, in order to heal, but I kept slapping Band-aids on it.

I'd fled to Europe two and a half years ago, and I'd been here ever since. After a few months of culture shock, I had found a good grief counselor and finally began to *feel* the loss. That first year abroad had been a messy, hard one. I'd come back to myself and had to confront not only the pain of losing Dillon, but also the hurt I'd caused in the aftermath. Namely, with Thatcher. My parents too, though I didn't feel I'd hurt them in the same way. I could acknowledge I had, but I honestly didn't care all that much since we'd never been all that close.

I'd felt the burden of what I'd done to Thatcher—how I'd wounded him. I *still* felt it. And seeing his handsome, somber face today had driven it home. All of what I'd done —to him and to myself.

I sank into my couch and covered my eyes. Thatcher. *Handsome* was truly not comprehensive enough of a word to describe him. The man was... astounding.

I'd liked him from the minute Dillon had told me about him and then from his first e-mail. The day I saw him in person felt like something out of a dream. Here was this guy who was positive, intelligent, charming, honest, gainfully employed, had a good relationship with his family, and he looked like that?

But now? It'd been two and a half years, and though he looked a little harder, he was beautiful. Appealing. He didn't necessarily look older, just slightly more seasoned. Maybe a little less naïve about the world. Though calling someone who'd served a year in Afghanistan and lost a close friend naïve was about the most condescending thing I could think of.

Therein lay one of the problems. *I'd* been naïve. I'd been so damn clueless about the world and my place in it. About how to live without my other half. So once I unstuck my feet, I ran.

What did this mean for me now? I'd need to talk through this with someone. I'd call Erin, my best friend, even still. Maybe, at some point, I'd even tell my old therapist about it. She'd wanted me to confront things with Thatcher. And, hey, I'd seen him. Done. Check. But I wouldn't see Thatcher again until I was able to talk to someone about him. Looking at him before I worked through the flood of feelings that threatened to drag me backward couldn't happen.

Even if I wanted to. Even if part of me, the part that wasn't terrified of becoming incapacitated from the emotions pulling at me, wanted to see him, touch him, and be near him more than it wanted air.

I just couldn't allow it to happen.

CHAPTER TWO

Bec

By the sixth meeting of the day, I'd lost my ability to focus.

Three weeks ago, Thatcher Wild had stood in my office. And though it had to be my imagination, I thought I could still smell the clean scent of his laundry detergent when I walked in and out of the room.

I'd slept fitfully every night since, waking before my alarm and surrendering to the fact that there would be no real rest so I might as well get on with it. I lived in a small, clean apartment in a town about twenty minutes from Kugelfels. I'd moved from Stuttgart—a significantly larger military base with far more resources and, well, everything.

So far, I liked Kugelfels, and I definitely liked the Education Center. Emily Wender, the Director of Education Services there, had been my boss at Fort Campbell.

She'd helped me get the job abroad through the GS—
General Schedule, or essentially what federal workers use—
system. My job at Fort Campbell's Ed Center had been a
GS position, which had been a major factor in my taking it
when I moved after I graduated. Once you were in the GS
system, it was much easier, or so they say, to find other jobs
and move around, then advance.

I'd tested the theory, and so far, it hadn't been wrong. I'd
loved my job at Stuttgart. Unfortunately, their contracts
were changing—the GS jobs were transitioning, like so
many were, to contracted civilian work. Somehow, Emily
had managed to finagle the Education Counselor job into
being a GS position when it hadn't been before. She'd
contacted me about taking the position and hadn't minced
words—it'd be much slower, a different pace. After almost
two and a half years of extremely busy workdays, that had
appealed to me.

I'd needed the non-stop meetings and conferences and
advisement sessions back then. Doing the work with my
grief counselor had required a lot of me. And staying busy
during the days had helped me feel I was using the time
well, like I hadn't necessarily paused my life to grieve. I
wished that hadn't been so important to me, but it had.

It also meant that by the end of my second year, I had
my ear to the ground about other opportunities. I was sad to
leave my counselor, and I'd made a few friends, but I'd
needed a change. And this time, I wasn't running away.

The move to Kugelfels felt so different than my move
overseas. I'd never stepped foot outside the US before
coming to Germany. I'd never really been anywhere or done
anything, minus a few trips during college for spring break
or family vacations, and those had all fallen within the

continental US. Well, until Dillon passed, and I traveled with my aunt. That didn't really count because all of those trips were shrouded in a haze and had been at a level I could never have afforded myself.

I'd left Clarksville, TN, the town outside Fort Campbell, on good terms with Ben and my dear friend Erin Flint —well, *now* Erin Flint. She'd married Reese Flint about four months after I'd left, and in one insanely long four-day trip, I'd made it back to stand with her for the big day.

But Thatcher, who'd been only good to me, if unbearably so...

I dropped my head to the desk in front of me and groaned with the memories of our last encounter.

"So, your day's going well." Emily stood in the doorway, a giant coffee mug in a manicured hand.

I straightened in my seat. "The day's fine. I finally figured out what to do with Sergeant Brooks, so he's all set."

She moved to the chair across from me, taking the seat with grace and poise, like always. "Good. Now what's with the groaning and head banging?"

With anyone else, I might've censored myself. Or, rather, with any other boss. Fortunately, Emily had known me at the absolute worst time in my life. We'd passed the boss-employee relationship way back then, and through her helping me get to Europe, then staying in touch and recruiting me here, we'd firmly cemented an actual friendship. Plus, as a single woman on a tiny military base in Europe, there tended to be a necessary connection.

Most women on a military base like this were Army wives. And that was great. In the same way that hanging out with married people when single could be less than ideal, joining a group of military spouses when you weren't a part of the culture proved challenging too. The military culture was a vivid and strong one, and I respected it so much. I straddled the world since I'd been a military sibling, and I'd been more connected to the Gold Star community in recent years than I might've been tuned in to the regular Army community if Dillon had gone on living.

All of that to say that Emily and I had bonded even more in our non-spouse status. She sat in front of me now, someone with whom I needed no pretense, and I wanted to tell her. I *needed* to talk to someone about this.

Before I began, her phone rang. She silenced it and stood. "Listen, you're coming out with me on Saturday. I'm doing dinner and going out dancing in Regensburg with my friend Summer and maybe one or two others. You're coming with, and you'll tell me everything then. No buts."

Then she answered the call and stepped out of my office, leaving me to my head-butting and groaning, along with a mild sense of dread and a healthy dose of antic-ipation.

"I love cheeseburgers," I said on a sigh.

"Me too. I've been single long enough I think I might marry cheeseburgers," Emily said, eyes fluttering shut as she chewed.

Summer Applegate nodded emphatically, her mouth also full of a large bite.

We'd met for dinner at a fancy chain burger place called *Klaus im Gluck*. I'd eaten at a few of their locations in Germany and had been more than happy to join Emily and her friend for the meal. Summer worked at the medical clinic on post, so I looked forward to getting to know her.

Even though Germany had burgers, not all of them

were created equal. Many times, they blended pork into the beef or added seasonings that weren't what we Americans thought of when we imagined burgers. *Klaus im Gluck* made excellent burgers, and even though it was a gourmet-style patty on ciabatta rolls with fancy aioli, their ketchup was good, and their sweet potato fries were mind-blowing.

Oh, and the cocktails. They had fabulous cocktails, of which we'd all partaken while waiting for our meal. I hadn't realized how much I'd needed a night out. I'd been in the area for six weeks, and this was my first girls' night out. In fact, the first of its kind in years.

After a few minutes of silence while we destroyed our dinners as though we hadn't eaten in a week, Emily wiped her hands and leaned back in the pale wooden booth.

"So. Spill. What's been going on with you?"

"Uh... like, since I saw you nearly three years ago?" I evaded, suddenly nervous to spill my guts about the situation with Thatcher.

Emily gave me her signature *you've got to be kidding me* look, which featured a single raised brown brow, perfectly shaped and completely effective at conveying any number of thoughts, including this one.

I sighed, then turned to Summer. "Okay, so I promise I'm not always a terrible person. It's been a rough few years but—"

"Stop prefacing. Summer is good people and isn't about to judge you. She, like all of us, has her own crap. So, tell us what's going on."

I took a fortifying sip of my cocktail, surprised to see it nearly empty.

"Do you remember Thatcher Wild?" I asked, his name on my tongue something both foreign and familiar.

"Of course. He was always around back at Campbell. Why?"

"He's at Kugelfels. We didn't part on the best of terms, and he stopped by my office a few weeks ago. It was…" My jaw pinched and my throat constricted.

"Oh, honey." Emily reached for my hand and squeezed, then turned and spoke to Summer, who sat next to her. "Bec and Thatcher were sort of dating before her twin brother died in Afghanistan."

"Oh no. I'm so sorry." Summer covered her mouth, her eyes wide.

I nodded to acknowledge her statement. It used to grate on me when people expressed their sorrow at *my* loss. As time passed, I'd come to accept that, often, when people said that, they meant it. I believed Summer meant it.

"So, you and Thatcher…" Emily prompted.

I decided to let it all out—to bring Summer in on the history, fill in the gaps for Emily, everything. "Well, to back up, Thatcher and I had sort of started dating. Then when Dillon died, I couldn't really handle… anything."

I took a drink of water, then set it back down. They both sat silently, waiting. The bustle of the restaurant around us and the lilting consonants of the German language and occasional laughter, all worked together to create a kind of privacy for which I was very thankful.

"I shut everyone out. Focused on work. He took it in stride, I guess. We never talked about it, and I never responded to the e-mail where he laid everything out for me before Dillon died. I just left it and never talked about it with him or anyone else. I couldn't."

Their faces, full of empathy, looked back at me. And for the first time in a long time, talking about this didn't hurt like I'd expected, especially given my reaction to seeing Thatcher. So, I went on.

"We fought before I left. He was so worried about me, and for the first time since I'd known him, he showed me something other than just calm, care, and concern. He begged me to reconsider, to think things through, and it infuriated me."

"Why?" Emily asked.

"I'd felt, for a while at that point, that he and our friend Ben were trying to step in as brother figures. And I both loved and hated them for that. But having it come from Thatcher, someone I'd cared about so much but *couldn't* be with... I can't even tell you how horrible I was to him. At the time, I felt totally justified and left without seeing him. He'd asked to see me. To clear the air, I assumed, and I just wouldn't have it."

I ducked my head, mind awash in the memories of my last words to him. The searing anger I'd felt, and yet, the desperate longing for him to just... *know*. To understand why I had to go without explaining it.

"What happened when you saw him at work?" Emily asked gently.

"It was awful. He wanted to get together. Catch up. I just said *no* and he left, clearly upset." My heart burned in my chest.

"I'm sorry, Bec. That sounds awful."

Summer tilted her head and spoke quietly. "Did you want to say yes?"

A glum sound masquerading as a laugh escaped. "That's the stupid part. *Desperately*. A huge part of me desperately wants to catch up and hear about his life. But the cowardly part of me knows that, when we do, I have to own up to how I treated him. Which means reliving some of those feelings and just... I don't want to have to go back there. At the same time, I know I need to—I *have* to. I've wanted to for years."

We all shared a sad smile, then Emily slapped the table. "All right then. It's time to move on. We're not staying in the sads. We're going dancing, and the time has come!"

CHAPTER THREE

Thatcher

The longest rotation of my life, then a hearty chewing-out by the XO, and now I'd been dragged to a bar or club or something by some guys who claimed to want to cheer me up.

I didn't need cheering up. I needed a heart transplant.

Bec Jones had been it for me since her first e-mail. I didn't know it then, of course, but that didn't make it any less true. Seeing her after years of missing her and hating myself for not hating her... *damn*.

She looked good, too. She'd been thin and burdened and weary the last time I'd seen her. It was a huge part of why I'd been so concerned about her choice to move overseas. She wouldn't just sit and talk to me about it. She got so mad.

My fist curled around the handle of a beer stein, the drink I'd been nursing for twenty minutes and the only one

I'd order tonight. I could tell Rob Waverly had come out to prove something, and the other guys were on the hunt for women.

I didn't need to hunt. I knew what I wanted, had known it for years. I'd tried with everything in me to shed the need for her so many times after Dillon passed. After she very clearly put me in a box labeled *Do Not Touch*. After she lied to me and left.

"Come on, man, let's see your moves."

Waverly beckoned, and I gave him a good-natured smile, then a head-shake refusal.

Waverly had been acting a little wild lately, like he needed to prove he could get back what'd been taken from him when insurgents captured him and Noah Miller in Afghanistan a few months ago. It hadn't been all that long, and he'd been stuck rehabbing a hand that wouldn't heal right. Something in him had changed. He'd started an intense physical training program about a month ago and claimed he was going into *phase two* with that, guided by the terrifying Sergeant Masters, so he'd be off all booze and late nights. He'd dragged me along for his last hurrah.

I hated not being game for it. I could dance. I loved celebrating with my friends and showing up for people. But tonight, like I had every night since I'd seen Bec weeks ago, I just wanted to be home.

"Hallo," a cheery, feminine voice said next to me.

I prepared myself, pasted on a courteous though disinterested smile. Small talk as a Black man in Europe could be interesting. Normally, it started with *"Where are you from?"* which was a very different question here than it was in the US. Often in the States, it had racist overtones. Here in Europe, everyone tuned in to their ancestry and lineage in a different way. Plus, in this case, I was actually a foreigner in a strange land, so to speak. But I wasn't up for it tonight. I turned to the woman, ready to brush her off, when I saw a face I knew.

"Oh, hey, Ms. Applegate. Out for a girls'—" I stopped, swallowing the words as I took in the woman's company.

Bec.

Oh, God. Bec in tight jeans and a blue top that would match her eyes if the low light of the place wasn't deceiving me. Even with her back to me, her hair longer than it had been years ago, twirling in dark waves to the top of her shoulders, I could tell it was her. I knew. I always knew. My heart twisted.

"Hey, Captain Wild." The woman's eyes blinked rapidly, then she tilted her head. "We're just out blowing off some steam. Small world, right?"

Small world indeed. Applegate was a nurse at the clinic on post. Kugelfels Army Base was a small enough post that everyone pretty much knew everyone else, or at least knew *of* them.

I smiled back at her, forcing my eyes not to linger on Bec like they wanted to, and spoke. "Sure is. Well, you ladies have—"

"*Thatcher.*"

The word—my name—emerged from Bec's lips on a whispered sigh-like sound and shot straight through me. The slow drip of adrenaline that'd started at seeing her became a full-on deluge.

She'd turned and stepped up to the bar, one hand on a drink, the other pressed to her chest.

"Hi."

"Hi."

Her voice came out breathy again, like I was some kind of vision—or maybe specter, more like.

And I wanted to turn away from her then. I willed myself to do it. To say *good to see you* and send her off. To dismiss her like she'd done me weeks ago, and years ago. To keep my distance and preserve some sense of dignity for my sappy little heart. But as so often happened when it came to Bec Jones, all the logic and strength I normally possessed fled the scene.

Summer Applegate had disappeared, and without my knowing it, I'd stepped closer to Bec and dragged my beer along the wooden bar top.

"You look gorgeous, Bec," I said, dripping oil into blue flame.

Her chest rose and fell like she took a big breath, though the bar was too loud to hear it.

"You look—" Her gaze slid over me, from lashes to lips, neck to chest, and a quick drop down before she swallowed and met my eyes. "You look so good."

Something I hadn't felt in years burst in my chest and raced along my veins to the far reaches of my body. *Desire.*

Whatever had happened in the last few years, Bec still at least liked the look of me. And maybe I could work with that. Maybe I could push her, just a bit, and get her to see what she'd done when she'd left and refused to even talk to me and treat me like a human.

No, not just a human. Like a man she'd cared for. Like someone who'd been through Hell and back with her, but who she pushed away like it was her job.

I elbowed the creeping resentment in the face and inched closer. "You out here looking for someone?"

She'd taken a sip of her drink, but when I asked this, she immediately started shaking her head, even before she set the drink down. "No. *No.*"

I wanted to smile at her emphatic words, though I still felt miles from that. Even so, I spoke my mind. "Good."

Her tongue slipped out and licked her top lip, then retreated, and she bit the same lip. A lip I'd tasted only a handful of times and admittedly thought about, even still. My gaze roamed her face—those deep blue eyes that looked nearly black in the bad bar lighting. Her dark brows thicker toward the center and thinning out to delicate little ends that I had to keep myself from tracing with a finger. Her slim nose, which now had a nose ring, and her currently flushed cheeks.

She looked good. So unbelievably good, and I wouldn't even allow my eyes to dip below her pointed chin and take in the rest of her like I wanted to do, like I hungered for. Because right next to my desire for this woman was a drum that beat just as loudly, shouting at me—*you can't trust her. She doesn't love you. You don't know her. All she does is hurt you and leave.*

"How—how's your night going?" she asked, her voice strained and odd.

"Going fine. Yours?"

"It's okay. But listen, I need you." Her eyes shuttered, then widened with alarm. "I mean, I need to *talk* to you."

Something about that slipup sent fire through me, and then it clicked. Bec was, at the very least, tipsy. I'd witnessed it only one other time, and for her, the faint buzz of two beers had been enough to open the floodgates of honesty.

Some distant voice in my mind smacked me upside the head and told me taking advantage of this situation was wrong. Another selfish and resentful voice pushed me forward.

"Had a drink or two tonight?"

She pursed her lips. "Maybe."

"You okay?"

"I'm fine, thank you."

I stifled a smile. Despite everything, I loved that sass. I hadn't seen it like this in too long.

"Of course you are." I leaned on the bar and dipped my head. She stood a full foot shorter than me. "You mentioned you need me?"

Her eyes narrowed. "I need to *talk* with you."

"What about?"

Her lips parted and drew my attention there. I breathed against the desire to lean down and kiss her. We were far from that. So very far from that...

She licked her lip again. "I just need to say some things."

"So say them."

Our eyes locked, and years, months, days, hours, minutes of our past compressed in my chest and jumped through my mind. Longing, aching, raging want and concern and hurt battled for prime placement. Like a battering ram to my ribs, her eyes bore into mine, and I lost my breath. I wanted to hug her, kiss her, even just touch her skin. I wanted to hold her and beg her and push her away.

"I can't."

Disappointment and worse, hurt, bloomed in my chest. I blinked, the fog dispersing in an instant. "Sounds about right. I guess it's time to stop expecting anything else, huh?"

Her face firmed, and she inhaled. "You know what? No. We're doing this."

I raised a brow. "What's that?"

"I'm tired of walking around feeling guilty and sad and like a terrible person for how I treated you. We're doing this." She glanced around. "But we probably shouldn't have this conversation in a bar surrounded by strangers where I have to yell and after I've obviously been slightly over-served."

My heart thumped, relishing the deep red flush at her neck and cheeks. "What are we doing?"

"I've got things to say, Thatcher." This time, her voice came out gentler and almost pleading.

And just like that, my anger and resentment evaporated. "Okay. Tell me when and where, and I'll be there."

CHAPTER FOUR

Bec

I didn't want to do this. I didn't want the shaking hands or twisty, knotted stomach. I should never have gone out with Emily and Summer. I definitely shouldn't have talked to Thatcher in all his tall, dark gorgeousness.

But the time had come. All my running away and then ignoring had caught up with me. When I'd messaged Ben to ask why he didn't tell me Thatcher was here at Kugelfels, he hadn't denied knowing we'd eventually collide. He'd said, *"Time to woman up."* I'd rolled my eyes and felt so annoyed I could hardly stand it, then had taken a moment to pause.

Because it was one of those times that reminded me of what Dillon had left me. He hadn't left me alone. He'd left me Ben and Thatcher. I might've run from them, and especially Thatcher, but they hadn't given up on me. Well, Ben hadn't, and maybe that was because I'd let him keep tabs on me by responding to him. And Thatcher hadn't given up on me—I'd pushed him so far away, he'd had no choice other than to leave me alone.

I'd told Ben and Thatcher once that I didn't need replacement brothers. And I didn't. I had twenty-three years of memories with Dillon, and I loved them all. Ben had become a close friend, and even though I'd been mentally cursing him the last few weeks since running into Thatcher, I could see his point. At some point, I had to confront this part of my life and what I'd done to a good man. That and a cocktail, and here I was.

So, I drove the ten minutes to a small café in the center of the town to meet the man I'd loved and lost because I'd left. It had felt like a loss, and one I couldn't control. I didn't always let myself think of him in that way—someone I'd loved. Denying it did me no good. Why pretend I hadn't had the depth of feeling for him when that was so much of why I couldn't stand to be around him after our relationship changed?

Facing him today was the least I could do. I owed him a genuine apology for how I'd behaved the last few years, and I hoped it would provide me the absolution to forgive myself for the same. *Wretched* wouldn't be too dramatic a word for the shame I felt just thinking about Thatcher. That had to be why just thinking his name caused my breath to stutter and my heart to speed. No amount of therapy had pushed me through that feeling. That might've been because I didn't allow myself to confront it. Even after I'd looked at the face of my grief over losing Dillon, I'd kept well away from the agony of knowing I'd hurt Thatcher. I'd blocked that out even more effectively.

I parked and took a moment to gather my thoughts. I could do this. It would hurt, but I could give myself and him this morning to clear the air, to repair a broken history, and then we could both move on from my cowardice. I couldn't have it any other way. We'd go our separate ways and then we'd be cordial, friendly even, when we ran into each other in the small community we now shared.

I exited the car and smoothed the pale green dress down my body to straighten out wrinkles. My brown purse matched my three-inch heeled sandals, and since it was a warm August day, I didn't have anything else with me.

I could do this.

I crossed the street, enjoying the planters hanging on every lamppost and bursting with pink, red, and purple flowers. Germans manicured their public spaces so well, and the little details like perfectly maintained flowers always reminded me how much I loved living in Europe.

"Bec," Thatcher's deep voice called out.

He approached from the opposite direction, and we met on the sidewalk in front of the café. He wore jeans and a light gray polo, the dark skin of rounded biceps peeking from under the sleeves. I smiled inwardly, pleased to see his penchant for polo shirts hadn't changed. They did excellent things for his arms and hinted at the torso beneath, which appeared even more muscular than it used to.

"Hey. Thanks for meeting me." My cheeks heated, an uninvited side effect of the flash of memory—how I'd been bold and tipsy on Friday and demanded he meet me. Hopefully, I'd be thankful for that boldness and not regretful when this was all over.

"Of course. I wouldn't miss it."

My heart sighed. There he was. My Thatcher. The strong, sweet boy. Or, more accurately, man. Because he was definitely a man.

"Shall we?" I gestured to the doors, which he stepped toward and then held open for me.

I gave him a small smile and moved past him to enter the building. In decent German, I asked for a table for two and the woman at the counter simply nodded. Thatcher followed behind, not touching me. A crazy jolt of longing for his hand on me—on my back, shoulder, maybe in my own hand—slipped through me, and I startled but hoped he didn't see.

The woman seated us at a small table in the corner. The café was part chocolatier and part bakery, and they served real breakfast and a basic menu for lunch as well. When Emily had mentioned it'd be close to my apartment, I'd suspected love at first sight, and I'd been right.

The inside was a peculiar mix of magenta and lime green, plus crisp white. It sounded garish, though somehow, it created a cheery, stylish feel. Upon entering, a large display case stretched the length of the wall, perfect little chocolate confections too beautiful to eat covering one-third. Baked goods nestled in baskets in the middle, and cakes took up residence in the last section. *Gorgeous.*

And speaking of, Thatcher sat across from me perusing the menu like we did this all the time. He appeared to be completely calm—all placid waters that I knew covered hidden depths. That I was sweating, stressing, so anxious I barely felt hungry, had to be broadcasting in my stiffness and expression. Though, maybe he didn't remember me any other way.

"Yes?" he asked, a smile in his voice.

"Huh?"

He set the menu down. "You were staring."

"I wasn't staring. I was observing." Covering the mortification of being caught ogling him and the riot of nerves in my gut, I tilted my head to one side. "Two entirely different sports."

He smiled then, one of his full, beautiful smiles. "Same old Bec, I see."

"You think?" My voice wasn't sharp or rough, but the words felt ragged coming out of my mouth. He had no idea how different and the same I really was.

His smile fell. "Well, I guess I don't actually know, do I?"

It wasn't a question—merely a sad statement of fact that reminded me why we were here. Neither of us could pretend this was all just a friendly catch-up. "No. You don't."

He nodded. Before he could speak, the woman returned and we ordered.

When she left, I took a big breath. "Okay. You ready?"

A cautious smile lit his eyes, but he only nodded.

Here goes nothing. "I'm sorry."

His gaze flicked back and forth between my eyes, his expression unchanging. If anything, it seemed a little distant. And obviously, he expected more than two words, which he totally deserved, but I felt small and weak here in my bouncy booth seat across from him and all his warm, strong beauty.

I summoned the strength I'd relied on—sometimes too heavily. "I left without saying goodbye. I'm sorry I didn't meet you when you asked. I was a coward, and I'm truly sorry. I've regretted that." *Every day since I left.*

He nodded again and swallowed. "Thanks. I regretted it too."

Though I didn't think he meant to, those words shredded me. "I'm so sorry."

We sat quietly then, though inside, my whole body fought against itself like my organs were attempting to rearrange themselves. My stomach ached. My heart and lungs seemed to be crushing against my ribs. I'd anticipated feeling upset, but I'd hoped I could keep it together better than this. I had more to say.

Maybe if I kept going, it would help.

"I want you to know that I did run away, but it was also the right choice. You worried it was running and that it wasn't good. I'll admit I was angrier with you for that than I should have been, and I didn't take the time to explain why I needed to go. Why I *had* to go."

His dark eyes watched me intently for a moment. "Okay."

A flare of annoyance shot through me. "Okay?"

He frowned. "What else should I say, Bec? I don't have all the pieces of the story. I don't know why you were my close friend and then everything went to hell and you pushed me away. So much so that you wouldn't even talk to me before you literally moved across the world. So while I'm glad to hear that the move was the right choice for you, and I'm sorry that I didn't understand at the time, I'm not sure what else to say."

His voice never raised or took on a harsh tone, but the words battered my already bruised heart.

"I'm sorry," I breathed out, feeling like a broken record.

He shook his head and rubbed a hand across his chin. "I don't want to spend the whole morning with you apologizing. Let's talk about something else for a bit."

Unease twisted in my belly. "What do you want to talk about?"

"How about you tell me what you've been up to since I saw you in Nashville two and a half years ago?" He squinted a little, then took a drink of the coffee that'd come at some point in the last few minutes.

I inhaled slowly, attempting to shift gears along with

him. I pushed away the objection, the *"how can we move past this to small talk?!"* on the tip of my tongue, and gave him what he wanted. I'd done that so seldomly, and I owed it to him to try. "Well, I lived in Stuttgart and worked at the Ed Center there until about three weeks before I saw you. I've been here for just shy of two months now, I guess? I traveled a bit, though strangely not as much as I thought I would."

"Why not?"

"Uh, well, I kind of crashed when I got settled. I mean, not physically, just... emotionally, or whatever. I finally started seeing a grief counselor and it really helped. It was exhausting, and between navigating life over here, trying to meet friends, and that, I didn't have a lot left for travel."

I cupped my cappuccino, needing the comfort of its warmth after that admission. I could talk about that time like this now, describing the surface details of healing without feeling the bottomless exhaustion and pain. But I still didn't like to.

"I'm sorry you couldn't travel. It sounds like taking that time was pretty important."

For some dumb reason, my throat tightened at his words. "Yeah."

He caught my eye. "I'm glad. And I know it's not my place, but I'm proud of you too. For getting help and facing your grief. That's not easy."

Something buried deep in my chest, down at my very core, thawed, cracked open, and sprouted. I'd never imagined he'd be so kind. That just showed what a self-absorbed idiot I was, because Thatcher, by nature and by choice, had always been kind and lovely. Far too good for me, for that matter, and my underestimating him just proved that.

"Thank you."

Our food arrived, and we shifted to discussing lighter fare. He told me about the last few years in his life—a company command at Campbell he'd taken as a brand-new captain, then the Captain's Career Course at Fort Benning in Georgia, then here, where he'd taken a second command in the OPFOR Battalion. As always, his resumé demonstrated his excellence, just like everything he did.

There was still distance between us—oceans and years of it. Inexplicably, recognizing that distance made my stomach clench and ache more than anything that'd happened so far today. It hurt, seeing it now, served right in front of me like my plate of salami and butterkäse.

We finished our meals, parting well enough. A simple "Thanks for meeting me," and his returning, "Of course. Have a good Sunday, Bec."

And then I got in the car and pressed the heels of my hands to my eyes and sobbed.

CHAPTER FIVE

Bec

Minutes later, a knock on the window of my car startled me so sharply I nearly shrieked. It served to silence my gasping tears, and I quickly wiped my eyes while looking up.

To find Thatcher standing at the car side, arms folded, eyes directed somewhere beyond my vehicle.

Oh. My. Good. Lord.

What was he doing here? And why did he have to see me like this? I didn't think I'd ever bawled in front of him. We'd never had a moment when I'd unloaded on his shoulder or even joined in when he and Ben cried at the memorial Dillon's unit held when they returned to Fort Campbell. Dillon had died a little over halfway through their deployment, just weeks after he'd come home for his mid-tour leave. I'd always be thankful for those ten days, and as time passed, I'd come to accept I was glad I didn't know they were our last days together.

The Bec of those years was someone who couldn't cry. I'd instinctively known that if I allowed myself to start crying, I'd do more than fall apart. I'd dissolve in my tears and disintegrate into nothing. So I'd locked away any outward show of emotion and used work, busyness, and anger to keep it away.

I wiped under my eyes, hoping I didn't look like a raccoon, and hit the window to roll it down a few inches. "Hey, Thatcher."

He widened his stance and leaned forward so his head dipped a little lower down and he could see me through the crack of open window. "Can you get out for a minute?"

"Uh, why?"

"Just get out, Bec."

My jumbled mind allowed the order, and I exited the car, not meeting his eyes. Just like Thatcher, always pushing a little, he demanded it with a hand at my shoulder.

"Come here," he said, his voice low.

I met his eyes then, just as he wrapped his arms around me and pulled me close. I held onto him, grabbing fistfuls of the back of his shirt, my head against his firm chest. Humiliation and grief warred for first place in my mind even as something in me loosened, eased. My heart bounced around my body and my stomach dropped, though tears jumped to my eyes again. Embarrassed and yet thrilled to be so close to him, my soul ached with the pain of our interactions ending so casually earlier, with how I'd left him before, and with the memory of grief that colored so much of the last few years. All that, and yet comfort marbled the moment. I didn't want to let go.

"I'm sorry. I don't actually sob uncontrollably in my car

all that often." I leaned away, realizing I might be wiping snot and mascara all over his shirt.

He looked down at me, one hand at the back of my head. His touch felt gentle but sure. "I'm sure you don't."

The warmth in his voice, his nearness, sent a sharp burst of longing in me, and I pulled back. I couldn't be feeling things like *longing* for Thatcher Wild. It wasn't fair to him, and it certainly wasn't fair to me. "Thanks. I guess I needed that."

"A hug?"

A rough chuckle escaped. "Well, yeah, that. And the cry."

His brows dipped low. "Can we at least be friends now? Can we swap numbers and just... not go another couple years before we talk again?"

And so we did. We shared numbers, and I got back into my car, only half tempted to cry again, the other half of me feeling oddly... light. I couldn't have him the way I really wanted—not as all mine. But maybe we could see each other now and then, and eventually, that wouldn't feel so much like a dagger to the heart. Just a slow bleed. And I could patch that up a little at a time. I could handle that.

"How was it?" Emily asked, stopping just inside my door Monday afternoon.

I saved the document on my screen, then slumped in my seat with a belly full of mixed feelings. "He hugged me."

Her eyes widened.

"When he found me sobbing in my car after we said goodbye." In what would live in my memory as one of the sweetest, most satisfying, and yet definitely most humbling hugs of my life.

"Wow."

I nodded. "Yeah."

"But... good? I mean, that sounds like you must've said some of what you needed to." She stepped inside and sat in the chair across from me.

I sighed, pushing away the flapping wings in my chest at the thought of the hug. Of being near him, period. "Yeah. Not all of it, but a good start. By the end, I just felt so sad and overwhelmed. The last half hour was all surface-level stuff about what we'd each been doing the last few years, our favorite trips since moving to Europe—you know, the usual stuff. I barely made it to my car before I lost it."

"Sounds rough." She crossed her legs and leaned an elbow on the desk.

"It was so many things at once, you know? Like, on one hand, it was horribly painful and the shame and guilt and all those feelings I'd worked through years ago came back in a rush. On the other hand, I felt... happy. Or, happy sad. Do you know that feeling? Like, I was so glad to be sitting there with him, and seeing him in person, and that felt *good*. But I was sad because there's still so much distance between us. And by the time I got back to the car, it just... all came out."

Goodness, did it. I hadn't cried that hard in well over a year. I hadn't allowed myself to feel anything about Thatcher in so long. Not until he came through my door weeks ago, ready to reconnect.

"I'm sure you were thrilled when he showed up again in the midst of that."

Emily's sympathetic smile reminded me she did know me pretty well. I was relieved someone here did. I'd been a very different person for most of the time we worked together at Campbell. Fortunately, we'd kept in touch, and she knew how I'd left—in a whirlwind and without a lot of time to say goodbye.

"You know I was horrified," I said, a chuckle escaping. "Actually, the hug that came after was..." *Everything.*

"He initiated it?"

I pressed my lips together and nodded, flutters of pleasure filling my chest. "That's just him. That's Thatcher. So kind, even when things are weird between us. I guarantee he noticed me breaking down on the way to the car and gave me some space, but couldn't resist checking on me. And when he found me, he couldn't stand to see me in pain. Even though I've caused him pain and been so dismissive of him, he worried about me."

And that reality had been too clear in my mind the last few days. I couldn't escape that embrace. When I closed my eyes last night, I'd felt him—tall and strong, the scent of his freshly laundered shirt and whatever soap he used. And far more than the physical, I remembered my heart loosening its death grip on my emotions. My whole being relaxed in that moment, slumping against him and clutching his shirt.

What the hell did that mean?

Emily, though she couldn't have known my thoughts, answered the question. "He's still in love with you."

My heart lurched and a thrill shot up my spine. Sharp, desperate hope moved from tepid pond to boiling hot spring in my chest. Though my greedy hands ached to grasp at that like a truth, I'd learned to keep the longing and need I felt for Thatcher under close, unyielding wraps. "No."

"He is. No one acts like that out of general concern, especially if you said you guys didn't part with plans to get together again." She lowered her chin and raised a brow like she wanted me to prove her wrong.

I couldn't give that idea a foothold. It was far too dangerous for my little beggar heart. "He's not. He did ask to swap numbers and stay in touch. I think maybe he wants to be friends, and I think I might want that too."

Something swirled in my belly. *Yes, I want that.* I wanted too much from Thatcher, and that gave me one good reason to stay away.

But the hug had thrown my determination to do so for a loop, and now, I had all kinds of crazy thoughts.

Thoughts? Never mind those. Let's talk about the feelings, woman. I had them. So many I could hardly breathe without feeling some new, pressing, precious thing. For someone who'd spent years feeling a hundred versions of blue, dusky grief, these new emotions were all sunrise oranges and pinks.

"You should. You absolutely should. This is a good man, Bec. I obviously don't know everything about him. Summer knows him from the clinic. I guess he's assigned to her doc, and so she's seen him for a few check-ups and referrals and things over the last year. She said he's polite and courteous, friendly and direct. He's always chatting with people in the waiting room. Anyway, point is, between what you've told me and his general reputation, I say *why not?* And more to the point? You need to do this."

A minuscule smile pulled at my mouth. Emily had *opinions.* It was one of many things that made her good at her job. It also made her awesome and yet challenging to talk with as a friend. She wasn't going to *just* listen. She would listen and then solve the problem, and usually, her suggestions were going to be right.

"I *need* to?"

"Yes. Because you've missed him. And I think he's

missed you. You have room in your life for a new friend." She wiggled her brows and then winked.

I laughed. The pressure valve in my chest that had held in the building tension brought on by just thinking about these things released, and with it, my unease. "I'll think about it."

She nodded, case closed, and left me.

Then she stopped by five more times before the end of the day to check if I'd messaged him. By the time I made it home from work, she'd texted me twice, and I'd decided I would reach out. I'd planned on it, though maybe not as soon as *today*. But Emily had lit a fire in me with the idea that I needed it because I'd missed him and he'd missed me and I had room for him.

I did. The more that idea settled, the more I found it to be true. And so, sometime after seven that night, I tapped out a text to Thatcher and hoped I wasn't making a mistake when I pressed send.

CHAPTER SIX

Thatcher

Bec had been on my mind.

Not that the woman wasn't usually somewhere in it, floating around and taunting me with her beauty and my unrequited feelings for her. Since seeing her the first time, she'd been front and center. And since holding her while she cried?

Nonstop.

So the arrival of her text sent satisfaction rolling through me. It was simple, but it meant she'd been thinking about me too.

Bec: *"Thank you for Sunday."*

Naturally, I responded immediately. I might've kept it together at our little meeting, but I hungered for anything she had to offer. It was why I'd turned around and tracked back to her—I couldn't get in my car and drive away without a plan to see her again. As sick as it might've made me, and as hollow as I'd felt at times with her, I still felt that pull. The magnetic force that drew me to Bec like I'd never felt with anyone before or since being near her.

I'd arrived at my car, opened and almost immediately shut the door, and walked toward the direction she'd gone. I didn't know what her car looked like or where exactly she'd parked, but there were only so many options in the small town's center. I saw a head covered in dark hair resting against the steering wheel of a white Prius, and I knew it was her. She must've shipped her car over—it was the same one she'd driven in Nashville.

And then I'd found her, and nothing on Earth could've stopped me from doing whatever I could to quell the tide of tears.

Me: *"Of course. Anytime."*

Bec: *"Nice of you. For the record, I don't normally do that."*

Me: *"Thank people?"*

Bec: *"Cry in people's shirts."*

I pushed away the uncomfortable thought that Bec might have someone she *did* normally cry with. I didn't want to think about whether she'd dated or if she'd had a similarly difficult time being with anyone else like I had.

Granted, we'd never dated—not really. We'd never *been* together, certainly.

Bec: *"Any chance you want to begin our friendship with a drink on Friday?"*

My pulse picked up. Any chance? *Any chance?* She clearly didn't know my level of desperation for her. *Good thing.* If she did, she'd be laughing hysterically at the absurdity of her question.

Sadly, I couldn't simply say yes.

Me: *"I start rotation tomorrow. I'll be free the weekend after Labor Day."*

Bec: *"Ah, right. I'm still getting used to that schedule. I guess let's put it on the books for that Friday? You choose the place since you've got seniority here."*

Did I fist pump into the empty living room of my apartment? Yes! Yes, I darn well did. I might've known better, but my impulse drove me to always be with her. It'd gotten me in trouble before, and I'd have to pray it didn't do that again.

~

The rotation went well, all things considered. As company commander, I managed over a hundred people, and when certain things went wrong, the job could be pretty stressful. The payoff was exponential. I'd taken a second command here at the training center because it gave me a chance to live in Europe. Plus, I liked a lot about command. Not always the stress of being the person to decide, though fortunately, Lieutenant Colonel Wolfe was a good battalion commander. He gave us a lot of support and, actually, a lot of opportunities for mentorship, which I ate up. I'd missed that with my first command and appreciated the effort he made to engage with the company commanders whenever possible.

The two weeks exhausted me, and I left work ready for a break and more than eagerly anticipating being with Bec. I wanted to get past the stiff, sad stuff. I wanted to hear something from her that would help me let go of the resentment I still felt despite myself.

Over the years, I'd justified her quick exit from Nashville and her ghosting me that last time we were supposed to meet. I'd made excuses for all of it. And from the sounds of her explanation weeks ago, I hadn't been far off.

What she hadn't addressed, not truly, was our history. The intensity of our initial connection and how it'd been trashed. I understood, or tried to, that she couldn't go back since her entire world changed when Dillon passed. For me, it was different. I'd grieved her brother, but I'd had room for other emotions, and my love—yes, love—for her hadn't ceased to exist merely because her brother did.

I hated myself when I thought that way, mostly because it was so selfish. But I wasn't a perfect man, and I *was* selfish sometimes. I'd stayed away from her, given her space, then tried to show up as the supportive friend or whatever she wanted.

I'd come to the sad conclusion that being around me, and maybe Ben too—though for some reason, especially me —had hurt her. And damn me, I resented that.

I mentally shook off that train of thought, which would bring nothing good. I didn't need to get all wound up about the hurt and sadness and *mess* of those years at Campbell, or the years after, right before I got to see her again.

I scooted a spare cardboard coaster back and forth on the bar next to my beer. I'd chosen a place inside a restaurant because, other than my night out with Waverly, I didn't really do the bar thing. I'd been anxious all day, eager to get here and see her, and also strangely dreading it if it meant more awkwardness and distance. What if she wanted to pretend everything was okay between us?

Or what if she didn't?

"Hi."

The voice interrupted my musings, and I turned toward it, familiar to me despite not hearing it nearly as much as I would've liked.

"Hey. Glad you made it." I smiled, the thump-thump in my chest accelerating with her nearness.

"I'm glad you suggested this place. It's gorgeous."

She bit her bottom lip and looked up at long blown-glass light fixtures and a copper-plated ceiling. It was an odd mix of industrial and old-timey. There had to be a more technical name for the style—it lacked the traditional Bavarian look, and beyond that, I had no clue what to call it.

"Yeah. It's cool. Different from a lot of places around."

Regensburg tended to feature Bavarian-style restaurants. That was a *great* thing, but I'd wanted something a little less... homey. I liked the show of this place, and the bar area gave off a cool, metropolitan vibe. My other choices would've been based on the food, and that wasn't what she wanted.

I'd only give her what she asked for—nothing more. That'd been part of the deal I'd struck with myself when I'd agreed to breakfast weeks ago.

"I like it." Her smiled seemed genuinely happy, and she squirmed into a tall bar-height chair next to me.

That movement, something about it, struck me as familiar, and a pang of nostalgia hit. I'd always loved that she was so much shorter than me. We'd never talked about it on e-mail, so it'd been a surprise. She'd been this tiny little package—like a little perfectly wrapped fireball.

If I'd thought she'd been perfectly wrapped years ago, I'd lacked imagination. Tonight, she'd arrived in a dark green dress, hair curled and loose to her shoulders. Her skin still held a warm olive tint, maybe a bit darker from the summer sun lately. On her feet, as always, were sky-high heels, and she still only came to my shoulder.

I studied her profile, admiring the slope of her nose and the curve of her lips. All of her curves, really, though I couldn't continue drinking her in like this much longer. She'd ordered her drink, the bartender had delivered it, and now she turned to me.

I shook the haze away and focused on her. "You look good, Bec."

Her eyes warmed, her gaze on my face a caress. "You too."

Then she ducked her head and sipped her cocktail.

I enjoyed a small burst of heat and angled my body toward her. "So."

"So."

"You've got me here. Now what?"

She chuckled. "Well, it's supposed to be mutual. We're supposed to be friends."

I nodded, silencing the *I'll never just want to be your friend.*

Her smiled faded though, and she licked her lips.

"I don't really know what it looks like. I hated the way we left things after breakfast the other week, just kind of *you go your way and I go mine.* I didn't like the last few years without you. I talked to Ben. Why couldn't I talk to you?" Her gaze flickered to mine, then back to her drink, and she took a quick sip. "So I guess I'm hoping this is the start of something new for us."

Thoughts swarmed my mind. A jolt of jealously at the news that she'd talked to Ben even though it *wasn't* news. A stirring of hope at the idea of starting anew, of there being any kind of *us.* And then a slow burn of shame for being so willing to take whatever she'd give.

But that last bit wasn't enough to keep me from agreeing. I cleared my throat. "Sounds good. I'm in."

Even if it made me an idiot.

CHAPTER SEVEN

Bec

I didn't typically believe in liquid courage. In fact, I sort of hated the trend to joke about "needing" wine or a stiff drink after a hard day or to gear up for a difficult task.

But I'd downed my cocktail—a very strong gin and tonic —in record time. On a fairly empty stomach. And now I watched in a kind of out-of-body experience as my hand floated out to Thatcher and touched his face.

His. Face.

Let's back up. He'd agreed to start over. *Yay!* And just that told me I'd taken the drink too fast—I internally cheered pretty much everything he did.

Thatcher seemed cautiously happy to be there. He'd chosen the place, so maybe he liked the atmosphere. He tended to be one of those *glass half full* types. He'd find the good in anything.

We'd chatted about our weeks—mundane stuff for me,

and he made the rotation sound fairly boring. Granted, when your job involved dressing in camouflage, zip-lining out of helicopters, and running around in the woods for weeks, it had a one-up on draggy Internet connections and slow talkers during meetings. It almost seemed like a game of pretend, the differences between our daily work lives.

By the time we finished our first drinks, we'd only grazed the surface. We'd ordered seconds, both of us had come by train and wouldn't need to drive, thank goodness. Not that Thatcher was in any danger of being even remotely tipsy—not at six-foot-two and just the right number of pounds to make him muscular without being bulky... sigh.

I couldn't keep my eyes off his chest. And his arms. He wore a long-sleeve, button-up shirt, which kind of blew my mind considering early September in Germany could be hot, and they weren't big on air conditioning. It was still fairly warm. My short-sleeved dress felt about right for the temperature, but sitting next to Thatcher made me feel hot.

I internally rolled my eyes. Could I be any more of a cliché? Probably not. Though honestly, I couldn't blame myself because the man was absolute magma. I'd thought so years ago, and it held even more true now than it had then.

"Bec?"

Thatcher's voice cut through my mental ogling.

"Yes? Sorry. What?"

"I asked if you wanted another drink?"

He tipped his head to one side and studied me, his eyes narrowing a bit as they did.

"Another? Uh, no... better not."

He blinked twice. "You okay?"

I smiled at his immediate concern. "Yes. I think I drank those two a bit fast."

He nodded slightly, then looked toward the bartender, as though to flag him for the bill. "Ah. I see."

And that's when I did it. I reached out, standing on the rung where my feet would've rested, and palm to his cheek, turned his head to look at me.

His brows rose, but I spoke before he could react much more than that. "Let's have dinner."

I didn't drop my hand, though. The feel of his cheek, smooth enough that he must've shaved before he came, and the curve of his jaw under my pinkie where it splayed wide on his face froze me in place.

What are you doing, crazy?!

His dark eyes didn't leave mine. He didn't pull away. No.

His hand lightly grasped my wrist, then slid up and pressed against where mine rested on his face.

My stomach dropped as heat pooled in my belly at his touch, the warmth of his large hand over mine, and the heady mix of sensual and sweet in the move itself. Nervous butterflies woke and took flight in my chest.

"Dinner sounds good."

My sanity returned and I nodded slightly, then pulled back. He immediately moved his hand, then smoothly stepped away to the hostess. Meanwhile, I stood on the ground, my heart sprinting. The feel of his warm palm on mine, pressing it to his face, seared into my mind.

The moment had been more charged, more thrilling and sensual and delicious, than anything I'd experienced. Ever.

Maybe I needed to get out more, sure. But... maybe it was Thatcher.

∼

The food looked and tasted amazing. The wine he chose was amazing. The conversation, amazingly, was amazing. And my brain broke.

Because I'd stopped being nervous as soon as we sat down and the waitress put a bread basket in front of us. I'd dived in with abandon, shoveling in two slices slathered in butter before I realized he was watching, holding back a laugh.

"Good bread?"

"Best bread."

When he smiled then, his eyes twinkled, and he looked so happy and pleased, my heart pulsed in response like it had a claim on that look and wanted it all the time.

We chatted about our favorite German food, and he mentioned a few local restaurants he especially enjoyed. I stopped myself from suggesting he take me to all of them, and soon. Because that press of his hand to mine, likely combined with my too-fast consumption of cocktails, had made me want things.

Time with him.

Dates with him.

Him.

No, no, no. *None of that, now.*

"What was that?" Thatcher asked, his fork and knife set neatly to one side of his plate.

"What? Nothing. Just... had a weird..." I trailed off.

"A weird?"

"An odd thought. Nothing, really. Anyway, so... what's next for you? How long are you here, and do you know where you go next?"

Bringing up Army plans always got soldiers talking about themselves. Thatcher didn't usually talk a lot about himself, and based on our last few encounters, that hadn't changed. Not that he wouldn't, but just that he was really adept at the conversational give and take and tended to give a bit more than take.

"Here for another year at least. I'll come up for my boards for promotion to major next year and that'll determine next steps." He fiddled with the coaster under his empty wine glass for a few seconds before asking, "You?"

"I'll be here for a while. I'm always keeping an eye on what else is out there. Emily brought me to Kugelfels, and I don't want to leave before I've been here at least a year, if not longer. So far, I like it, and I think the slower pace will be good for me. I'm hoping I can travel a bit more than I have lately."

He nodded. "Do you still travel with your aunt at all?"

My breath caught. Something about his nod or his tone seemed too careful. I'd traveled every weekend I could after Dillon died. My aunt was ridiculously wealthy and lonely since my uncle died years ago. We'd never been close before, but thankfully, she seemed to know I needed an escape and had taken me with her whenever I could go. Ben, Thatcher, and even Erin had expressed concern that I traveled too much, avoided the grief, etc. They were right, but it was how I managed then.

"Not much, no. She's in Singapore semi-permanently now for something with her job or... something. I don't know. Once I moved to Stuttgart and started trying to deal with things instead of ignoring them, I didn't say *yes* for quite a while. And eventually, she didn't invite me anymore."

It'd stung at first when I'd realized we'd been using each other. I wasn't sure it was all that wrong, but it probably wasn't healthy. In the end, I'd taken the steps I'd needed to in order to get healthy.

"Ah. Well, I'm glad you did what you needed to do."

"Me too."

We sat quietly as our plates were cleared, then perused the dessert menu. I'd stuffed myself silly with bread and then my main meal, a delicious salad with pancetta, chicken, vegetables, squash blossoms, and lettuce. I'd mainly been eating pizza and schnitzel, so I'd jumped at something different. It had been so satisfying, though I regretfully turned down dessert.

We left the restaurant at half past nine, and I didn't realize until then I'd be cutting it close to get to my train. It turned out Thatcher needed to catch the same one, so we hustled through the city on foot until we had tickets in hand and reached the platform just as the last express train to our town arrived.

"So we're in the same town, too. What a small world," I mused aloud as we slumped into seats. I was relieved to be sitting after the near-jogging pace we'd set to avoid missing the train.

"Definitely small. Much smaller when you add Army life and working on military bases into the mix." He smiled and elbowed me jokingly.

"True." I sighed and registered what a satisfied sound it was. As the darkened landscape slipped by outside the windows, I regretted that our time together would end soon. And I didn't want it to be over. "I had a lot of fun tonight."

"Me too."

"We should do it again," I said as we stood when the announcement for our stop came.

We stepped off the train and onto the platform, then walked to the sidewalk in front of the station.

I nodded to the left. "I'm this way."

His brows rose and fell. "Me too."

We turned and walked together, not quite touching. Though I'd started wishing he'd put his arm around me, both because the windy evening had brought with it a chill, and because I wanted him to touch me again. It felt more like a need now, and I couldn't blame it on the fog of a cocktail.

"Are you going to the fest next weekend?" he asked after a few moments of quiet.

"Oktoberfest? In Munich?" I couldn't really imagine Thatcher wanting in on that madness.

"No, no. The local fest. The battalions usually reserve tables for Oktoberfest, though. If you want to go, that's probably the best way to do it if you haven't before." He shoved his hands into his pockets when I stopped walking at the corner near my building.

"I think I'll skip that one this year. Have you gone?"

He laughed, a bit incredulously, and nodded. "Yes. It wasn't my scene. I drank too much, felt terrible, and yet still managed to be the most coherent person and had to physically carry a guy to the train. I can check that block and never go back."

Of course, he'd been responsible even when he'd overdone it. But that wasn't like Thatcher, and based on the small frown, he'd probably felt terrible for it. He could let loose from what I remembered, but he didn't see inebriation as a sport, especially after the trouble Ben had after the deployment. Just that small observation, the slight crease around his mouth, made me restless for more of him.

"I can imagine. This one is here, right? The small fests are usually the best anyway."

"They are. I'll be there Saturday night. I can text you what time. I'll be with a group, and you're welcome to come." He smiled, all kind and genuine.

"Sounds good." I waved and stepped away before I ended up crowding in and hugging him like I wanted to do.

I went to bed that night feeling something I hadn't felt in years. I looked forward to seeing him again and was excited about what might be in store. I'd gotten over the dread of the future, over the guilt of *having* a future when Dillon didn't have one. For the first time in so long, I felt anticipation for what might lay ahead.

CHAPTER EIGHT

Bec

I hadn't worn my dirndl in about a year. I'd put on a little weight, and frankly, it now looked even better than it did before.

I'd left the US underweight. My appetite after losing Dillon had been absolutely nonexistent. It wasn't healthy, and I'd tried to make myself eat when I could. Occasionally, I'd feel hungry, mostly when Erin cooked for me or made me snickerdoodles. I'd been weak and thin. I'd gained weight, gained strength, gained in so many ways over the last few years, and it felt good. I'd never had curves before, but I did now and I *loved* it.

I wondered if Thatcher had noticed. I knew he liked my face. My body, both from being nearly five years older than when we met, and probably nearly twenty pounds heavier, was rather different.

If he didn't, then oh well. Because *I* liked it. I felt at

home in my body in a way I hadn't before. And the cinch at the waist, the sweetheart neck of the white eyelet blouse, and the tight girdle-like style of the dress did remarkable things for me.

"Well, we look fabulous," Emily said, sweeping a finger under her eye in the mirror of my bathroom while I slicked on some lipstick.

"We do indeed."

A few minutes later, we had our purses slung over our shoulders and were walking up the small hill toward the fest tent. The town's *Festplatz* was essentially an empty lot since the castle at the center of town was too small to accommodate the set-up of the large fest tents that could hold hundreds of people.

"Summer's meeting us there?" I puffed out a breath as we approached our destination, feeling winded and anxious.

"Yep. She'll be about thirty minutes behind us, so she said to save her a seat."

Emily's burgundy and black dirndl looked great on her, and I admired the perfect bow on her right side as we walked.

I'd also tied my bow on the right side, indicating my status as a single woman. Heaven forbid we put the bow on the left and put out the "taken" vibe. The bow symbology had been drilled into me by the brisk woman at the *trachten* traditional clothing store I'd visited about a year into my time in Germany.

The large white tent loomed, music blaring already. The energy of people slowly filing in infected the air and created a buzzing excitement. Emily must've felt it too because she glanced at me, her eyes bright, and we both laughed, happy to be there together.

It'd been a good week—I'd helped some soldiers figure out how to use their benefits, which motivated me to keep doing the job. There were a lot of frustrating and seemingly pointless days, but when I actually got to solve problems for service members, that made it worth it. I was learning that the pace at Kugelfels moved *much* slower than the previous Ed Centers where I'd worked. Passing the time between appointments and meetings could become oddly challenging sometimes.

Happily, the last few days had been relatively busy. The intervals between rotations became the best window for soldiers to deal with things like education concerns, so we'd had an uptick.

A few minutes after arriving, we found a seat at a mostly empty fest table. These long, fairly thin tables were made of wood and covered with a shiny lacquer, though they were often so worn from years of use they looked old and even stripped. The benches were thin wood planks about eight inches wide, the legs of the benches and tables metal. Since we'd arrived on the early end, we'd lucked out finding a well-situated table near the middle of the tent where we could reach the bar and see the stage. Soon, there'd be no way to move around without sliding sideways and begging *entschuldigung* as you went.

Thatcher had texted and said he and his friends would be there soon. I hoped we'd manage to keep the table long enough for them to arrive. We spread out, taking up as much space as possible, and when a harried waitress came around, we ordered beer and pretzels. I focused on these tasks rather than let the nerves fizzing in my belly take over my entire body. Though I'd tried to calm the desire to see Thatcher all week, I couldn't deny that existing in the minutes before being near him again made me feel like I might crawl out of my skin. I'd never thought of myself as particularly impatient, but this was next-level inability to wait.

We people-watched for a few minutes, a decent distraction, before I remembered what I'd been wanting to ask Emily. "Did I hear you telling Jackie that some guy had taken five language tests in one week?"

Her head whipped around and she raised one dark brow. "Yes. And let me tell you, I had my doubts. We have rules about this kind of thing, and he scheduled them weeks ago *in person* with Donna. No idea how he talked her into that. When I saw the schedule for the week, I nearly flipped."

Donna ran our testing lab and administered all kinds of tests for the community, including DOD language tests that resulted in higher pay for soldiers when passed with certain scores. She'd taken leave this week and next, so Emily had stepped in to run things.

"I can imagine."

"So I get all geared up to tell this guy, *sorry, no can do*. I made a plan to spread out his tests this week into next, and I had them all blocked off. Then he waltzes through the door wearing a button-up shirt and slacks with nice leather shoes and a beard. No lie."

My mouth opened in shock. "He's a contractor?"

"Nope. Active duty."

"What?"

That didn't add up. Regulations required US soldiers to be clean-shaven except for certain special operations groups. Emily had already told me how much she liked having other NATO forces on post because the Brits and Italians could have facial hair and she loved the combo of a beard in uniform.

"Yep. His info checked out, and he promised me he'd pass all his language tests without issue. He said if he didn't pass one, I could use it to justify canceling the next day's test."

"And you let him?" Emily believed in rules and regulations. It was one reason she'd been so successful in the GS system. The news that she'd bend a policy, much less retell the story in this odd, gleeful manner? Truly perplexing.

"I did." Her eyes widened. "He put me under some kind of bearded, linguistic-genius man spell, and I said *yes*."

I laughed and paid the waitress after she plunked down two large glass steins full of golden beer. "A *bearded, linguistic-genius man spell* does sound very hard to resist."

She shook her head like she, too, couldn't believe it. "I know. I mean, it was. He was... incredible."

I could *not* believe what I was hearing. "Seriously?"

"Seriously. He passed them all, no problem. Written and spoken. No. Lie. And then he thanked me for working with him, all kinds of humble. It was... I can't even..." She slapped her hands flat on the table. "Honestly, it was the sexiest thing I've ever witnessed in my life."

I laughed full-out at that. "I can imagine that was your special form of catnip."

"If ever there was one made for me, it was him."

"So, did you get his number or anything?" I asked, engrossed enough in the story and the mystery of Emily's perfect man not to let my eyes wander around the tent searching for my own version of perfection.

She frowned into her drink. "Sadly, no. I couldn't do it without seeming insanely unprofessional, and I felt like that would just... ruin it."

"I'm sorry. Maybe he'll be back? Maybe he'll track you down."

She wrinkled her nose. "Doubt it. That's okay. I kind of like knowing he exists out there somewhere, speaking perfect French, German, Spanish, Arabic, and Pashto, wandering around in his fancy leather shoes and his perfectly trimmed beard. Plus, he's probably super arrogant and rude and a total desk jockey type."

I let her have the brush off, but before we could say anything more about the bearded mystery man, a hand brushed over my shoulder and Thatcher bent to say hello.

"Hey, Bec," he said, a broad smile on his face.

"Hey." And then I stood, wrapped my arms around him, and hugged him. Like it was normal. Like we greeted each other that way all the time.

My body did the things my mind wouldn't let it. If I'd had the *thought* before, I would never have permitted a hug so quickly. We'd only hung out twice, and the first time had been awful. I'd been looking forward to seeing him with an almost desperate anticipation, so having him here meant my cool was officially dead.

I let him go and he stepped back, the same grin lighting up his gorgeous person. I would never get over the sight of him—ever. He just... well, he did it for me. Always had. And just because we'd struck up a tenuous friendship, at best, didn't mean I didn't find every single thing about him attractive.

"You guys have room for us? We've got six—seven, counting me."

He scoped the table, and Emily and I both nodded.

"Of course. We were saving as many seats as we could. I couldn't remember if you'd told me how many you had with you. Please, sit down." I waved them all toward the table and sat too, then Thatcher plunked down next to me.

Bodies shuffled around us and found seats. I looked at

Emily, now happily flanked by men in lederhosen, and swallowed at the realization that Thatcher wore them as well. My eyes shot to his lap next to me, then I whipped my head to the other side of me, heat crawling up my neck and into my cheeks.

"There's Summer," Emily said, nodding to the corner of the room.

I popped back up and smiled when she spotted me and headed our way. "Can you guys make room for our straggler? She's just arriving."

Two men nodded, one smiling agreeably and one seeming notably stern, and then they slid to the side to make space for Summer next to Emily.

Thatcher made introductions, and normally, I'd retain the names of the four men and two women in his group, but the music had amped up along with the noise from the crowd, so it required anyone not immediately next to me to yell. That, and Thatcher's arm was sandwiched to mine, our bodies pressed close now that more people had claimed spots at the long table.

Being this close to him, practically smashed together, made my skin feel hot and my heart fluttery. I wished I'd ordered a water. Instead, I sipped my beer and hoped it'd cool me down. And then Thatcher leaned down and spoke into my ear.

My eyes shut at the feel of his breath and the sound of his rich voice so close, delectably close, and particular enough that I'd know it anywhere. We chatted back and forth like this, simple exchanges about our weeks, and something sparked to life in me.

After another while—which was as specific as I could get because the atmosphere in the tent was so cheery and buoyant, I hadn't looked at my watch since we first walked in—the band started a certain song and the whole tent let out cheers and stood. Thatcher held out a hand and I took it, then we both stepped up on the bench. Germans and some Americans sang along, and those of us who didn't know the words clapped and danced and laughed.

We stood and danced song after song, the air thick and hot. Thirst pawed at my throat, and as the next song played, my breath came up short and the edges of my vision grayed and narrowed, but I blinked it away. Thatcher glanced at me and smiled. Then someone bumped him from behind and he grabbed my shoulders to shield me. Our bodies crushed together and my hands were on his chest, our faces close enough that if I tipped my chin up just slightly, our lips would touch.

His dark gaze captivated my attention. The pounding bass and clapping hands, and general celebratory raucous energy pulsing around us, faded. I licked my lips, wishing my mouth didn't feel so dry, wishing my dress didn't feel so tight. *So tight.*

Strong hands found my waist, then I moved down but didn't fall. Thatcher ducked his head and looked into my eyes once our feet touched the ground.

"Come on, Bec. Let's get some air."

With one hand around my shoulders, he walked us out the exit and into the cooling evening air. I sucked in a breath and let it out, my head swimming.

"Did you have too much?" he asked, a concerned frown on his beautiful face making him look so handsome and appealing. If I'd had any breath left, it would've caught.

"No. Half a beer. I think I just overheated. Let me sit for a few."

He steered me to a bench, and I sat with my eyes closed and breathed slow and deep.

Minutes later, he sat next to me and pressed a cold glass bottle into my hand.

"Drink."

My mouth found the straw, and I pulled at the liquid. The water tasted heavenly, and I didn't stop until I'd downed half the liter.

"Thank you. Sorry." I would've been embarrassed if I'd had too much to drink and he'd had to haul me out, but that wasn't it. I didn't feel good. I felt really bad, actually, and it had nothing to do with the half a beer I'd had over the last few hours.

Though, come to think of it, having half a beer and nothing else couldn't have helped matters. We'd planned to get half chickens and pretzels, but I'd gotten caught up with Thatcher and then the singing and dancing and had completely forgotten to eat.

Now there's a sentence I haven't said in years.

I shook my head and sighed audibly. "I'm an idiot."

"Be nice to my friend."

I eyed him, a funny smile on my face matching the wobbly, soft feeling in my chest. "What?"

"I said *be nice to my friend* because you said you're an idiot, and I happen to know, with certainty, you're not."

I blinked a few times, the kindness and concern in his voice, yet again, making my heart pinch. "You're too sweet, Thatcher."

"Nah. You are, and always have been, too hard on yourself. I see that hasn't changed." He raised a *no denying it* brow.

I huffed, then grinned. "Me saying I'm an idiot when I behaved like an idiot isn't being too hard on myself. That's being realistic. I nearly passed out because I overheated and haven't eaten in hours. I'm old enough to know I need to eat regularly, or even that I need to take a break and get some air."

He shook his head. "I think that's called being human. And look—here you are, outside getting some air."

"Yeah, but you had to help me."

His eyes narrowed and he looked away. "No big deal."

The warm and friendly exchange ended abruptly. Was it the memory of that heat, the little flame that lit when he'd caught me and we were so close to pressing together and banishing all the space and history between us with a kiss?

I didn't think so. Whatever it was, he'd withdrawn. And after the soul-deep joy his kindness and care had showered on me moments ago, the distance felt dark and painful in a way I couldn't have imagined until I felt it now.

CHAPTER NINE

Thatcher

T his was a bad idea.

Bad idea. Bad idea. Bad idea. The words bounced around my evidently empty skull as I walked next to Bec. Alone. _In that dress._

After she'd mainlined the water and cooled down, we'd gone back to the tent for a few minutes before she'd leaned in and said she was leaving. And like the fool for her I'd always been, even after our earlier exchange and the dose of reality that'd come with it, I'd decided to go with her.

She'd shimmied around bodies and pulled Emily and Summer down, yelled in their ears that she was leaving and gestured to me, likely saying she'd be fine because I'd walk home with her. It was after ten at night, and though it was a small, safe town, I liked that her friends wouldn't have let her go alone.

They knew enough about me to feel confident I'd get

her home safely. Of course Summer knew me from the clinic, and I'd known Emily years ago, at least loosely. I wasn't a stranger, and they knew Bec wasn't an idiot.

Now, we walked side by side in silence, the autumn Bavarian air crisp and the sound of the fest still thumping in the distance with the bass beat of the band.

"You were right. It's a good fest." Her voice emerged scratchy and a bit strained from yelling.

"It is. I like that they let everyone dance and get a little crazy. It never gets out of control. I'm sure that's why you can't stand on the benches in Munich. People get absolutely obliterated, and I can only imagine the injuries that would result in fools standing on benches and trying to dance around like that."

She chuckled low. "It sounds like you really love Munich Oktoberfest."

"Yep. One hundred percent my favorite. Second only, probably, to Masters, who loves it." I thought of the quiet man and wondered how he could even stand to go to stuff like that. Few events were less fun than being the only sober guy in a group of busted idiots.

"He's the one who was next to Emily? Real serious-looking and left an hour in?"

"You noticed him, did you?" I eyed her surreptitiously.

She laughed. "Is it possible *not* to notice him?"

"Don't know what you mean," I said, feigning ignorance.

She pulled me to a stop. "Seriously? The man is like... like..."

A twinge of jealousy jabbed at my gut, but I shoved it away. I crossed my arms and planted my feet. "What's he like, Bec?"

She rolled her eyes and started walking. "You've seen him."

"True. And I can see how he's... eye-catching." Dude was ripped in a way normal people weren't. And he was a good-looking guy too. I could see the physical appeal for sure. "So you're into that whole *male fitness model Adonis* look, huh?"

She turned enough for me to see a small smile as I hustled to catch up with her. Then she surprised me by putting a hand on my wrist, halting us.

"I can appreciate it, sure. But he's not my type."

The intensity in her dark blue eyes made my stomach clench. "No?"

She shook her head back and forth slowly, and her gaze dropped to my lips. My heart, already racing, tripped into an all-out sprint.

"What's your type, then?" I sounded normal. Maybe a bit gruff. Not lightheaded or weak or completely hopeless like I felt.

She stepped closer. "You know for a fact my type is—"

"Bec! So glad we caught you! Are you feeling okay?"

Emily's voice broke through the moment, dispersing the taut energy but doing nothing to calm the thrumming of my pounding heart.

Bec stepped back and twisted her hands in the strap of her purse. "Yeah, just worn out, I think."

Emily trotted up next to her and slung an arm around her waist, urging them both forward. Summer fell into step beside me.

"Sorry we interrupted," she said quietly.

I forced a good-natured chuckle. "No problem. Not sure you really did."

We walked along quietly, Emily and Bec weaving back

and forth as Emily regaled her with a story. When we arrived at Bec's building, I stopped at the corner.

"See you ladies soon. Have a good night."

Bec didn't smile or respond—her meaningful look spoke for her. She had more to say, and man, did I want to hear it. But I wouldn't get to tonight.

"I'll walk with you. My car's another street over." Summer hugged Emily and Bec and then shuffled along next to me for half a block. She reached her car, and I waited with her on the quiet street as she unlocked it.

"Thatcher."

"Yeah?" I turned to see her standing in the open door.

"We did interrupt something," she said gently.

I nodded and with one last wave, rounded the corner to my street. She was right, and I'd likely think of nothing else until I knew exactly *what*.

I slipped inside my place, careful to keep my footfalls light. The older man who lived in the apartment below had never complained. But I'd lived in a first-floor apartment at Campbell, and the people above me had been mercilessly loud. I never wanted to be that kind of neighbor.

My phone buzzed just as I settled into bed.

Bec: "*Make it home ok?*"

I shut my eyes and let the memory of her flood in. Her intense dark blue eyes. How her gaze dropped to my lips, and just that had lit me on fire. The neckline of the dress arcing over her curves, which I admittedly admired more than I probably should have. The aching need that shook my hands just before Emily interrupted us.

She would've kissed me. I knew she was going to, and I'd wanted it. I'd been greedy for Bec for the better part of a decade, and that hadn't changed.

I blinked up into the dark. Where could it go? Where

would she want it to go? Was I just a convenience? Someone who knew Dillon and what she'd been through? If that was the case, would that be so wrong?

More than that, she'd reminded me of one of many issues we'd have to address if we wanted to continue being friends, let alone anything else. She'd said, *"yeah, but you had to help me,"* like that was the worst thing she could imagine.

It was too much like running away. She hadn't wanted help or concern or care. She hadn't wanted me.

I groaned and grabbed the phone. No way would I be able to fall asleep without responding.

Me: *"Yep."*

I'd leave it at that. I'd...

Without my permission, my fingers tapped out. *"Great seeing you tonight. Thanks for walking me home."*

I pulled a pillow over my face and yelled into it, then let it flop back next to me just as my phone lit up with a returned message.

"You walked me home, but even so. You're welcome."

I shook my head. "The sass." I'd always loved it. It was one of the first things that came across in her e-mails, in fact. She was sassy and scrappy and funny. Even when she was hurting, she'd been funny.

She'd also pushed me away. So far away. And then she'd run. I couldn't pretend I didn't understand, and I could see how good it'd been for her. She'd gotten help and worked through her grief, and more than anything, I'd wanted that for her.

Yes, I'd also wanted things *from* her, but I wasn't an idiot. I recognized she'd have nothing to give until she'd worked through those hurts. It made sense that she needed time. I'd expected her to need years, but I'd also expected to be able to help her through. To be there. As someone who'd loved her brother, and who... yeah, I mean, why shrink from it? Who loved *her*.

But she'd run fast and far and didn't look back. How pathetic that I'd take her dark looks and her nearness now, even when her apology hadn't changed a thing. She meant it—she felt sorry. I could see it and hear it and *feel* it, but it didn't change the fact that she so easily ran across the world, and the only reason we reconnected came down to a chance meeting. Wasn't that sign enough for me that she didn't feel, and never had felt, the same?

Maybe I'd call Ben. He'd been with me through everything that happened and all the years after, especially after he got out of the Army and had no one to worry about beyond his sisters, me, and Bec, who apparently e-mailed him every so often, and sometimes even called. Well, and Whit Grantham, his super country star girlfriend turned wife, but still. He knew Bec, and he knew me, and he'd said *nothing* about her moving here. We were past due for a chat.

CHAPTER TEN

Thatcher

Ben didn't answer.

I let it ring probably ten times. No luck. Granted, he had a hugely pregnant wife, and they might still be sleeping. Shoot. I'd hoped to catch him before I had any more time to think about Bec.

I'd awoken to a text from her. She must've sent it last night, and I had been too caught up in my mental rabbit chase to see it. Probably best. It said, *"Dinner tomorrow? I'll order in."* And that was all it took for my mind to sprint back to her, to all the things that might happen if we had dinner at her place.

I scrubbed a hand over my face and grabbed a sweatshirt, my keys, wallet, and phone. If I couldn't talk to Ben yet, I'd get in a long run and hope that distracted me. Luckily, my phone rang before I made it out the door.

"Well, well, the Consort of Country has deigned to call me back."

"The Queen of Country made me," Ben said through the phone, sounding fakely irritable.

"It's good to hear your voice, man." I dropped to the couch and stretched out.

"Likewise. It's been too long."

"Agreed." It'd probably been more than two months since we'd talked. We texted periodically, but calling made a difference.

"So, your message sounded like this was more than a catch-up call."

"How long have you known Bec took a job here?" No sense in putting off the reason for calling.

"Ah. Yeah. Only about two months, actually. I didn't know last time we talked. She mentioned moving a bit before that. I didn't know she was at Kugelfels until she was *there*. You and I hadn't talked, and... well, I wondered if you'd even see her." A thin thread of guilt wound through his words.

"I've told you how small it is here."

"Yeah." He stayed quiet a moment, then let out a breath. "Yeah. And I guess part of me hoped you guys would run into each other and be forced to talk."

I laughed humorlessly. "Well, mission accomplished."

"Really?"

I could picture him, blue eyes bright and a pleased smile on his ridiculous face, which no doubt sported some obnoxiously bushy beard now that he was out of the Army.

"Yep. And long story short, she almost kissed me last night, and I wanted her to."

He chuckled. "Sorry to break it to you, but none of that is a surprise."

Irritation surged. "It's not? A woman who disappeared from my life coming up on three years ago, who—let's face it —ripped my heart out when she left, shows up at my duty station in the middle of Germany without warning, trips over an apology or two, and now I'm ready to just... take whatever she'll give?"

"You're talking to a man who accepted a fake relationship in order to be close to the woman he liked. So I may not be the best person to give advice."

I sighed and scrubbed a hand over my head again. "I need your help, man. You know us both."

"What's the problem? Lay it out for me like I'm clueless."

I sat up and rested my elbows on my knees. "I like her. I'm pretty sure I still love her. Definitely, parts of me do. And I'm still angry—resentful, even. It's too messed up."

"How does she seem?"

"She seems good. Not like a whole new person or anything, but she's already talked openly about grief counseling and how her first couple years in Europe were focused on working through some of those issues."

"Sounds like what I've heard from her too. She's been working hard and deserves a lot of respect for where she's gotten to now."

I shut my eyes, smashed them closed. "I do respect her. I do. But I don't trust her. And yet, I'm over here barely containing my happiness at her suggesting we get dinner tonight."

"Ooh. Sounds like a date."

I shot to my feet, eyes popping open. "Is it though? Kind of sounds like it, and man, last night she would've kissed me if her friend hadn't interrupted. What does that mean? How can I trust that she's not going to run away from me?

And how can I be with someone who had my heart in her fist and just threw it away?"

Ben made a tsking sound before answering. "I'm sorry, man. I think you know it wasn't simple carelessness that created her need to escape, and I dare say it wasn't even mostly about you."

I plunked back down, guilt and embarrassment souring in my stomach. "I know. *I know* that. I don't begrudge her the need to deal with things how she did. I wish it could've happened a different way, without her cutting me out entirely, but whatever. I get it mentally, even if it still feels... crappy."

"It *was* crappy. That's the thing. It feels crappy because it was. I've told you, Erin and I both told her she needed to at least e-mail you. I never did get why she wouldn't. But I know this—Bec's a good woman. One of the best. And if you want to see what's out there for you two, then do. That doesn't mean you have to take her scraps. Get her to talk to you, and not just surface-level apologies. You know her in ways other people don't because you were there through some of her darkest days. My guess is, despite her flight to Europe, she trusts *you*."

I nodded along silently as he continued.

"It's okay if you don't trust her. Part of dating is figuring out if you can trust the person. I argue that Bec is worth the effort and is most likely trustworthy, but *you* have to decide that. If it comes with some... physical bonuses while you do figure that out, well, good on ya."

"That easy, huh?"

"No, not that easy—worth it." His serious tone drilled home the point.

I knew he was right.

"How does she look?" he asked quietly.

"Fine as hell," I said miserably. Ben's laugh filled the speaker, and I couldn't help but join him. "Seriously. She looks good. *So* good. Like she sleeps now, and eats, and feels things other than rage and sadness."

We both sobered at that.

"That's good. It's nothing but good, my friend."

"Truth," I agreed.

He cleared his throat then. "I think you should let yourself enjoy being with her. And when you have those thoughts about the past, talk about it. I'm guessing she's done a lot of apologizing and you haven't said much about how *you* handled those few months."

I narrowed my eyes in suspicion. "You're *guessing?*"

"Or I may have been informed."

I slapped the couch next to me. "Come on. You've talked to her? Recently?"

"Yes."

"Tell me!"

"No."

"Dude."

"Sorry. If I spill all my secrets, Bec will kill me. Not to mention Whit would key my car."

I made a *pshh* sound. "Whit bought you that car."

"*Hush.* Point is, you haven't done much giving in the give-and-take of a conversation about hard things. It's time to think about that. I get that you need time to adjust to even seeing her in person, but she'll need to know how you feel if she's going to apologize or deal with what you perceive as her wrongs against you."

I hugged a throw pillow to me. "That sounds like I'm a little crybaby."

"Having human emotions doesn't make you a crybaby. Being someone who cares about people and feels things when they get hurt makes you great, Thatcher. It doesn't make you weak. What'll make you weak is if you cling to all those negative feelings and miss a chance to be with someone you've loved for nearly as long as I've known you."

That landed like a punch to the gut. "Damn, Ben. When'd you get so wise?"

"When I stopped drowning my sorrows, avoiding my feelings, and got help. You were my voice of reason more than once—probably a hundred times then. Let me be that for you now."

I exhaled a long, slow breath. "I hear you. I'll do my best."

"Good."

"Yeah. So, tell me about impending fatherhood and work and marriage and all that. Also, did you tell me Bea just moved to Europe?"

I'd met his extremely introverted sister a few times over the years. An overseas move for her struck me as insane, though it didn't surprise me she'd do something a little unexpected and throw everyone for a loop either—she might've been shy, but she always had that little spark in her eye.

We talked for another half hour before he had to go. We said our goodbyes, and I took a moment to thank God for Ben Holder. He was a good man and a great friend, and the closest thing I had to a brother. No offense to Camilla, my older sister. Truth was, I'd grown up wishing for brothers. When I met Dillon and Ben at twenty-two, I'd found them.

I wouldn't ever presume to have felt the hardship of losing a brother like Bec did, but I had grieved. Deeply. Though very differently than she or Ben had.

Talking to Ben had given me focus and gotten me out of the useless merry-go-round of fears and anger I'd fallen into last night. I could be with Bec and see where she wanted things with us to go—if anywhere. And I could try to admit how I'd felt and how I'd handled her disappearing. I didn't want to make things worse, and I wanted her to be happy. If she wanted to be with me, even as my friend, I couldn't let these feelings swallow me up.

CHAPTER ELEVEN

Bec

He knocked on my door exactly on time.

I smiled even before I opened it, anticipation and happiness that he'd agreed to come an energetic mix pumping through my veins.

"Hi, welcome. Thanks for coming," I said, practically breathless with excitement.

I'd nearly kissed him last night on our walk home. And, *oh*, how I'd wanted to. I'd never been less thankful for Emily, but I'd accepted it was probably best I didn't actually go for it. He'd seemed more than interested in the moment. Though, in truth, there'd been several other instances that'd spoken to mixed feelings about me. *Us.*

What I had realized in blazing relief? I did want an us. I felt ready for an us. I didn't know to what extent. Rather than fumbling my way into an ambush kiss on a street corner, I figured maybe a better idea would be to talk about it like adults. Over dinner.

"Thanks for inviting me," Thatcher said, stepping through the doorway and handing me a bottle of wine. "Hope you still like pinot noir."

I smiled down at it, pleased to see nothing had changed. He always had such good manners and was so thoughtful. He was just so *good*.

"Perfect," I said, then walked farther in and set the bottle on the kitchen counter.

"This place is pretty different than the last apartment of yours I visited," he said, eyes drifting around the small, tidy room.

I chuckled. "Not hard to beat that crap-heap me and Dillon had, is it?"

He smiled, then winced. My heart twisted at the silence and his expression. "You can say his name, you know. I can talk about him now."

He swallowed and nodded. "I'm glad."

"Me too." I pulled out a wine key and began opening the bottle. "It's a relief not to want to curl up in a ball and cry every time I think of him. I have no idea how I ended up staying in Clarksville so long, living in the apartment we shared, and yet couldn't even say his name."

"I'm sorry it was like that."

He kept his eyes on the bottle as I tipped it and poured us each a few inches of the garnet wine.

I set the bottle down and handed him a glass, then held mine out toward him. "To healing and progress."

He touched his glass lightly to mine with a *ting*. "To hope."

Yes. That said it perfectly. I couldn't see where things

would go with us, but maybe there could be an us. I wanted to know, and I *hoped*.

A knock on the door broke the moment as we both drank to the toasts. I couldn't tell whether I was relieved or irritated, though I settled on relieved. I didn't totally know what I was doing—what I aimed for here. Well, I wanted to be with Thatcher. It felt good. I wanted to be around him and close to him. I wanted to have him all to myself.

Now that I'd gotten him here, he was so much more than I'd remembered. Stupid thought considering he was an insanely good-looking, tall, kind, wonderful person, and I'd always been mentally and physically affected when he came near. Still.

I grabbed the bags of take-out from the delivery man and thanked him, offering a euro for a tip, which worked out to be about a dollar. Whenever I did move back to the US, I'd sorely miss the tipping conventions here, which amounted to—*we pay our employees well enough, we don't need your charity.* So, in most cases, a euro or two per person at a nice meal, or less, was more than enough.

"Oh, you got Karla's." Thatcher's voice sounded pleased.

"You like it? It and the Italian place are the only two I've tried. I thought I remembered you like Indian food..." I swallowed the end of the word, a flutter low in my belly shifting me off course.

I hadn't mentioned the *before* time much at all. Not just before I left—before Dillon passed and Thatcher and I were growing something together. Something that, even at the time, had scared and excited me because I knew it was special.

"You're right. I do. Thanks for the thought."

"I just got like five different things and naan, and I can't even remember what else. Evidently enough to get a free bottle of wine thrown in, so we've got backups if we need it." I held up the freebie bottle.

He chuckled and tore into one of the bags, pulling out clamshells of piping-hot food. "I don't recommend the free wine unless you want a searing headache tomorrow."

I gasped. "What? You're telling me it's not good?"

He shook his head. "Sorry to break it to you, no. They don't give away their best wine. I'm guessing it's about a euro at a store."

"Yum," I joked.

We worked side by side, setting up a little buffet line of take-out containers and then served up plates full of delicious food. Chicken korma, mango shrimp, tikka masala, curry, and several other dishes I didn't even remember ordering.

After sampling each of the dishes, we settled into casual conversation. I promised myself a celebratory high five at some point because I'd managed not to be weird or awkward thus far. I didn't exactly feel awkward or weird, but I felt like my *feelings* were. A bit, anyway. Like I'd walked into the room and half of me had run to one side, and the other to the opposite wall. I'd metaphorically ripped in two, and though it wasn't an unfamiliar feeling, I was surprised and pleased I hadn't made Thatcher uncomfortable with the back-and-forth of my thoughts.

I liked him. *So* much. I wanted him. *Soooo much.* Those feelings terrified me, and so did what they meant. Yet he was here. I'd pushed away all those fears enough to get him here.

"What's been your favorite place to visit?" he asked between bites.

"Probably Budapest. I really love that city, and I didn't

expect to. Not that I expected *not* to. It just wasn't a place I'd always dreamed of going, so it surprised me. It's vibrant and friendly, and the food is *so* good." I'd only taken a handful of trips outside of Germany, but it stood out among the rest.

"I have heard Budapest is cool. I haven't been yet, but it's on my short list."

"Ooh, what else is on your short list?" Excitement swirled in my chest at the thought of travel, and particularly, him traveling and seeing new things. Maybe even what it would be like to see him in those moments.

"I'd like to see Scotland. I've been to Rome but I want to see Pompei. I went to visit Verdun, and I'd like to go back to Normandy. Top of my list is probably Barcelona. I—"

"Wait, really? Barcelona?"

He smiled, his brows pinching. "Yeah."

"That's always been on my list."

His smile faded, just a little. "I know."

Heat poured out in my chest, warming me and quickening my heartbeat. "You do?"

He nodded. "I remember you saying it in one of your e-mails. I'm surprised you haven't gone yet, though."

More than his gorgeous face or the taut muscles of his chest and arms or the sound of his voice, more than all of that, his memory of our interactions years ago made my stomach clench and my hands ache with the need to touch him. I searched his eyes, my heart galloping, and belatedly registered he'd said something that merited a reply.

"I'd planned to early on, then decided I wanted to go when I could be..." My words faded away as the frantic chaos in my chest and the drive to press my lips to his swarmed my mind and made it hard to think.

"Could be..." he prompted, his head canted to one side, watching me closely.

"Happy." I licked my lips, then took a sip of wine, the admission a little like taking off my shirt and tossing it in his face.

When I looked up from the wine, on which I'd focused completely as I took the drink, I found him with a heart-breakingly soft look on his face.

"That's a good idea," he said, his voice low and just like his expression—soft.

I nodded. "I'm going for my birthday this year."

He sat back, and a grin grew on his face until he outright beamed at me, a smile so glorious someone needed to memorialize it in a photograph and blow it up to put on the side of a building. My heart clenched at the sight and the sentiment behind it.

"That's amazing, Bec."

My throat ached as emotion crept up, threatening to spill out. I clamped my lips closed and nodded, then looked away for a moment to gather myself. "It is."

He just smiled in return, and the emotion and pure joy at sharing that progress with him, at him knowing the significance of my willingness to do something celebratory on my birthday—on *Dillon's* birthday—loosened the words from my mouth before I had a second to think about it. "You should come."

He blinked.

"I mean, it's a whole group going. Well, at least, there's like three of us and a few more thinking about it, apparently. The flights are insanely cheap that weekend, and it's a great time to be there, though I really don't know why, but—"

"I'd love to go with you. I mean, as part of the group. I'd

like to celebrate you, and obviously, I want to eat my body weight in paella."

I laughed, a little forced, but not false. "You really should. Here, I'll send you my flight confirmation so you can find the same one."

I hopped up and grabbed my phone to shoot him the e-mail, wondering if this would prove to be the best or most idiotic thing I'd ever done.

While I messed with my phone, he began clearing the table. We didn't talk much more for a few minutes as we shuttled dishes to the kitchen and I put leftovers in air-tight containers for the fridge. He stood at the sink and watched water fill one side with bubbles. The only drawback to this apartment was the lack of a dishwasher.

"Hey, you're a guest. You can't do the dishes." Not exactly good hospitality to put my dinner date to work.

He looked over at me with a plate in one hand and the scrub brush in the other and raised a brow. "Watch me."

I huffed, though I couldn't hide my smile. *Dang*, he was cute. Even with the kindness, the memories, the thoughtfulness, and the general glory of his physical form, the cherry on top of the absolutely mouthwatering sundae that was Thatcher Wild was his adorableness.

And it was high time I did something about it.

CHAPTER TWELVE

Thatcher

Bec bustled around behind me, sliding leftovers into the fridge and wiping down the table. No matter where I heard her, I could've sworn I felt her eyes on me.

In fact, I knew I did, because Bec's eyes on me had never felt light or playful. They'd always felt like a purposeful, slow stroke over my skin. She'd given me a few of those looks—the kind that made me question my manners and want to grab her and take her mouth, her body, for my own.

But I wouldn't do that. If anything was going to happen between us, it needed to come from her. At this point, I hoped to God it would. Like, I'd literally and actually said the prayer in my head, forgive me.

So when she leaned her back against the counter right next to where I stood at the sink, sliding the last of the dishes to the other side, my pulse jumped. My hands held her attention where they rinsed the suds from the plates, then my skin.

"I love your hands," she said on a whisper, like she couldn't help the words from escaping.

I froze, the warm water running for a second, two, three, before I shut it off, turned to her, and in one movement had a hand at her lower back and another at her face. I had to bend to reach her, and she'd gone up on her toes.

She must've grabbed for me the same moment I did her because her arms were around my shoulders, then at my neck. Our lips met and it felt *right*. So damn right and long overdue. And more than that, it felt so good, I could hardly think past the slide of her lips and the tentative touch of her tongue.

The goodness, the rightness, the sheer pleasure of her mouth and body made me groan and wish we could get closer. I pulled back to see the color high on her cheeks and her lips still parted from our kiss. I smiled, even with the heavy pulse in my chest that said I more than liked this woman. So much more than liked.

"How are you still so short?" I asked, distracting myself from those heavier thoughts, then reached down and hoisted her onto the counter. She inched back, laughing, and I stepped forward, flush with her body, and angled her head to kiss her again. Deeper. More.

Her hands clutched at my shirt, and she pressed herself into me, the feel of her body soft against my chest delicious and pure temptation. I wanted to touch every part of her. Taste every part of her. Know every part of her.

And that stilled my hands, stopping them on their steady course from her face to her waist. I pulled back, just slightly, and rested my forehead against hers. I'd never held that pose with anyone—being that eye-to-eye close had never appealed to me with anyone but Bec.

"Damn, woman."

She chuckled, then turned her head and placed a kiss where my neck met my jaw. I swallowed, and she kissed along my throat where my blood thrummed and raced. She was driving me out of my mind—I was utterly mad for her— and if I didn't stop it soon, I wouldn't remember why I'd done so in the first place.

I stepped back, extending my arms, hands at her shoulders, to put space between us. "No more of that."

The confusion on her face looked good-humored but genuine. I swallowed, waiting for my pulse to slow and my words to return. Imagining grabbing her and hauling her with me to the couch occupied my mind. While I stood there, not speaking, her face fell and she blinked.

"I'm... sorry." Her voice shook, and her shoulders slumped.

I reached for her, setting a hand on one of her thighs and lifting her chin with the other. "No. Please don't say that. I'm sorry for leaving you hanging."

She pressed her lips into a smile, and I sighed, frustration with myself leaping in my chest. "Seriously, Bec. I'm slowing down because of me, not because of any other reason. Certainly not because I'm upset about kissing you."

Her brow smoothed just a little. "Okay."

"I'm an idiot," I muttered under my breath.

"Don't talk about my friend like that," she said, then placed a warm palm to my cheek.

I swallowed, desire and joy surging in me. I laughed, too, because of course she'd bring that back to haunt me. "Fair enough."

I held her wrist and inhaled slowly, impressing the

moment into my mind. She looked... maybe still upset a little? More like serious and overwhelmed. I couldn't blame her.

"Oh, Bec, I missed you." I dipped my head to kiss her lips, just a quick one, and then stepped back between her legs to hug her.

She hugged me close with arms and legs, head on my shoulder, and the impact of her wrapped around me felt a little like heartbreak. It wasn't, of course, because heartbreak was all brutal and enduring, and this was a cocktail of emotions—pleasure, relief, joy, sadness, regret.

We let go and I stepped out of the embrace, knowing if I stayed close, I'd end up kissing her again, and I needed to not do that. Not before we'd talked a few things through.

"I missed you too, Thatcher. More than you will ever know." She swiped a finger under one eye, then the other.

I noticed darker patches on several places along the sides of her fitted shirt—marks where my hands had been. "I got you all wet."

Her eyes fluttered and her mouth opened. "Uh—"

"Your shirt. From the dishes. My hands were wet. Sorry."

The grin cracked her face, and then she laughed. Full-on, free and real laughter that flipped my switch, and I joined her. The tension that had crept in—from the kiss and my fumbling through trying to slow myself down a bit, and the emotions of her statement—bled away as we enjoyed this new moment.

"I should go," I said after we'd caught our breath.

"I guess you should." She gave me a bright smile, though, and it sent my stomach to my shoes. "When will I see you again?"

"Rotation starts this week, so I'm pretty much working until early October."

"Oh... yeah. Sometimes I forget." She frowned.

"We can text, though. It's not great, and service is unreliable, but I'll see anything you send when I do get service and can check in. Then maybe we can get together once or twice before the Barcelona trip. If you really think I should come."

She bit her lip, then said, "I do. You should. And yes to the texts."

We'd moved to stand by her door. I hadn't brought a jacket since the mid-September night was mild enough and my walk home would be short. I'd *just* kissed her, and yet didn't quite feel like I could just... dive back in for another one, however much I wanted to.

Fortunately for me, Bec had never been the kind of woman to wait around for what she wanted. I reached for the handle of the door, but she grabbed my arm, stepped close, and urged my head down with a hand on my neck. Happy she'd taken charge, I obliged and pressed into the kiss. It was short, far too short, though better that way at this point.

"I'll see you soon."

"Let me hear from you. When you can. Just... whatever works."

I nodded and stepped out of her apartment, relishing her words. The fact that she wanted to hear from me and even stumbled over herself a bit... it felt good. In fact, the whole night had felt good—the conversation and meal, the clean-up, and definitely the kissing. Good grief, I could kiss her forever. I'd thought it years ago, and nothing had changed, though the impact of our physical connection was only hotter and more complex.

Walking out into the cool night air, I reflected that it was right to stop the progress of that heated moment, though. As much as I would have loved to carry things further, I couldn't wade in more physically without some clarity emotionally. And we hadn't gone anywhere near that. I'd hoped maybe she'd broach the subject. Still, we'd had such a good time. I didn't want to turn the mood to our past and all the hardship and sadness that lay there.

I didn't want to forget it. I wanted to move on. But I'd need her help to do it.

CHAPTER THIRTEEN

Bec

I didn't want him to go.

It felt wrong that he should leave after lighting my fire. Even his attempts to douse it in logic and *cooler heads prevailing* talk didn't calm the flame of desire he'd fanned.

I leaned against the door, my fingers finding their way to my lips. My eyes fluttered closed as I remembered his touch, the warmth of his hands, and the command of him. He was a friendly, kind guy, but he'd been pushy and definitely in charge during the kiss.

And, oh, I liked that.

Then he'd stopped, and it hadn't just been a break. It'd been a full stop. I wish I could say I understood why, but I didn't. He'd said it was him, not me, and I didn't know what that meant. It had to be at least partly me.

We were breaking through the ice that'd frozen over

between us the last few years. I couldn't reasonably expect that to happen all at once. Even if I really just wanted to move past all this and get to... to... what?

I slouched through the apartment, getting ready for bed and deciding on an early night. It wasn't even late—he could've stayed for a movie or something. Though, to be fair, I wouldn't stop wanting to touch him, and he likely would've had to keep pushing me away. My pride wouldn't last long against that, even if he did claim it wasn't because he didn't want me.

I needed to understand. If we were going to keep seeing each other, which I hoped we would, we needed to address that whole situation.

I plumped the pillow under my head, currently failing at its job to provide comfort, and then punched it a few times. I didn't want to have to wait weeks to see him again. I didn't want to wait for anything with him. He was everything I'd wanted for so long but didn't let myself think about or even dream about—not that I'd always succeeded at keeping him out of my dreams.

I'd convinced myself years ago that I'd left him behind, and if I ever did see him again, even after counseling and better understanding him and the situation I'd left, I never imagined he'd want me back.

I needed to understand him, and I'd have to be the one to ask—to push a little. And I had a few weeks to figure out how.

"So, tell me, tell me." Emily sat down across from me at the two-man table in the break room.

"It was great," I said, though a twinge of... something... plagued me.

"Yeah? That's convincing."

"I'm just... still thinking about it. I don't know. I'm angsty, and I'm not good at being angsty anymore, I guess." I bit into the pastry I'd picked up at the Bäkerei on the way into work this morning.

"You're angsty about Thatcher? Like how you feel about him?" Emily sipped her newly brewed mug of coffee.

Could I explain the issue? I needed to try because maybe saying it out loud would clarify it for me, too. "No. Or... yes? I don't know. Honestly, I'm not like this. We had a great time, and I want to see him again, but I can't help feeling—"

"Excuse me." A tall woman peeked around the corner into the room. Her brown hair spiraled around her face and ended at her shoulders. She wore slacks and a white button-up shirt.

"Oh! Katie!" Emily jumped up and extended her hand to the woman.

"Hey. The sign said to come back and then the woman in the testing office pointed me over here..." She gave an apologetic smile.

"No, my fault completely. I lost track of time. While we're here, let me introduce you. This is Bec Jones," Emily said, a hand toward me. "And Bec, this is Katie Miller. She's going to jump in as our admin since Cindy had to quit."

I extended my hand and shook hers. "That's great. Nice to meet you. Are you new to Kugelfels?"

"I am. I just moved here about a month ago? Maybe just over. I've been getting settled with my husband who has been here... a while."

Emily's eyes widened. "He adjusting okay?"

Katie nodded.

I smiled, confused by the tone in Emily's voice. "I actually think I met him a few weeks after I started this summer. Is his name Noah?"

Katie's smile beamed. "Yes, that's him."

"He's great. Seems really focused on nailing down his bachelor's."

Katie nodded. "He is. I know the time in Afghanistan threw things off a bit with his semester in the spring, but he's back on track."

"He's doing great," I said, because from what I'd seen the guy was a rockstar, managing courses along with work, and apparently a family too. Good for him. So many soldiers juggled their jobs, education, and family, and it always amazed me, even though it'd been my job to help them do it for years now.

"Thanks. Well, I'll go have a look around the reception desk and let you two finish. No rush."

"I'll be right there. And, actually, I've got someone coming in to train you for reception in about a half hour." Emily smiled, and we watched Katie head back out.

I wondered why Emily didn't go right with her. A few seconds later, she tilted her head to the side, and we walked to the farthest corner of the small room, away from the exit.

In low tones, she spoke. "Noah Miller is one of the guys who was captured."

A spike of alarm shot through me. "What? When?"

"On a TDY to Afghanistan in the spring. He and another guy were taken by the Taliban and held for a week."

"Holy crap. How did I not hear about that when I met with him? Or when I got here?"

I sifted through my memories, looking for anything in

them that would've pointed to his going through such trauma. He'd never said a thing. He'd taken a semester off due to the scheduled TDYs, and thank goodness he had. Underneath those practical thoughts, my heart pumped with adrenaline.

"I think everyone in the community thought it'd be better to move past it once they were recovered. Noah's a good guy. I couldn't believe she wanted to work here, but it's great for us. He's been geo-bachelor until very recently." She shook her head.

"Well, it's great that she's here. And that we can support her and help her adjust." The words came out easily while my chest constricted and pressure piled up in my head.

Emily scuttled out to get Katie settled, and I slumped back in my seat, staring sightlessly at the half-eaten pastry. No appetite anymore.

Captured. I swallowed. My throat worked without success. I took a drink from my coffee, willing it to magically solve the closure.

Dillon hadn't been captured. Dillon had ultimately been shot. It wasn't the same thing. *It's* not *the same thing.* And Thatcher. Thatcher had been there. *No. No. No. Ignore.*

My elbows dropped to the table, and I held my head in my hands, eyes closed, and focused on my heartbeat. Steady. Too fast, but steady. Dillon was gone, but Noah Miller had made it home safe. He was safe—I'd seen him after all that, and I never would've known. Everyone was home safe.

Thatcher.

My frantic mind pushed *him* to the fore. Would he ever travel to Afghanistan again? Would he deploy there again?

For that matter, *had* he deployed there again? What the hell was I doing with someone who could be killed the same way my twin brother had been? How could I possibly sign up for being close to Thatcher when I knew the wreckage that could be caused—and that'd been family. I didn't know what it would be like to lose a partner, a lover, a spouse. There was no point in comparing because, either way, it was horrible and brutal and *wrong*.

I'd chosen to continue working in a military community, even after I left Fort Campbell. I would be lying if I said part of my motivation wasn't that being close to the Army life made me feel connected to Dillon in a small way. Like, if he had lived, we'd still be near each other. And that I helped men and women like him, so it'd make him proud if he knew about it.

I crushed my eyes closed even tighter. I'd worn mascara today, which meant tears and crying were not invited. I exhaled slowly, counting beats before inhaling. In... two... three. Out.. two... three.

After a few minutes of calming myself and sipping now cold coffee, I chucked the last of the pastry, to my deep regret. I turned off the break room light and returned to my office.

I had work to do. I could think about all of that mess later. Thatcher wasn't in Afghanistan, and I didn't know if he ever would be again. More than that, we weren't together. We'd had a nice time last week. I didn't need to start thinking about him like we'd made commitments. That would be the definition of premature. *Don't borrow trouble.*

I locked down all thoughts of deployment, Afghanistan, mourning, grief, fear, Thatcher... I had a meeting coming up and needed to focus. If the pulsing behind my eye concerned me, or the clench of my jaw caused the ache to intensify and reminded me of my evasive mental gymnastics in the past, I didn't let it concern me. I wouldn't ignore all this forever, just... right now. Just this minute.

I had work to do.

CHAPTER FOURTEEN

Thatcher

I attempted to stand straight, but that made my head feel like someone had taken an ax to my brain.

The knock came again, and I shuffled more quickly to the door and opened it. There stood Bec, looking sweet and soft, concern ringing her eyes.

"Wow. You look miserable."

Her beautiful lips, which I very regrettably couldn't kiss, turned down.

"Flattery." My throat hurt too. Probably allergies. Might've been a cold. Whatever. It had come to murder me in the hours of last night and ruined all the plans I'd been dreaming about for the last few weeks of rotation.

"Can I come in? I brought soup and some other stuff." She held up a baggy with something in it.

"Yes, please come in. Just don't touch me and get sick. I don't want you to be sick for your birthday next week."

I held the door wide, and after she walked in, I pushed it closed. It clattered shut with a slight bang—I didn't care. It saved me from having to move my body in order to shut it.

I crossed my arms and shuffled over to the couch, then flopped down. She'd never been to my place before, and I didn't have the ability to host her. How could I when the claws of this virus or cold or super allergy had me in its grips?

She made an *aww* sound like she pitied me, so I raised my head an inch to look at her where she stood, unbagging things on my kitchen counter.

I grunted out a "What?"

"You're a super pathetic sick man, just like Dillon was."

She said it in a way that *sounded* sympathetic, but the way she pressed her lips together to hide a smile meant otherwise.

"I am not pathetic. I'm actually sick. I feel terrible."

She didn't respond, and I didn't say anything because, as I mentioned, my body had betrayed me to the illness.

A few minutes later, Bec sat on the edge of the couch next to where I lay. I opened my eyes and found her smiling down at me.

"Here's soup. You'll have to sit up and eat it. I put it in a mug so you don't even have to summon the strength to use a spoon." Again, her voice came out gentle, but those words...

I narrowed my eyes at her and frowned. "You're mean."

I sat up and she handed me the soup, not letting go until I held it with a solid grip. I sipped it, and the savory warmth soothed my throat.

"Maybe you're nice," I amended.

She chuckled. "You're kind of a sad sack, which I have to admit is making me so happy."

I shot her a look while taking another drink of soup.

Once I swallowed, I had to ask. "Why would that make you happy?"

She bit her lip, hiding another smile, which should've irritated me. In the end, I felt too tired to care. Plus, even in my state, I could appreciate the beauty of her delighted face, of her straight white teeth pressing into her full bottom lip. I'd always loved how she did that. I'd only seen it in person a handful of times, but it was often the smile I pictured her with—one she tried to hide but just couldn't.

She set a hand on my arm and stroked her fingers along my skin. It felt so, so good. She should do that all the time— she should always touch me. I would make a rule that when she was close by, she had to touch me.

I watched her caress my skin, my eyes drooping a bit in pleasure until she squeezed my arm and I looked up to see her smiling at me.

"You are so steady and strong. You're always composed and together. I've never seen you... undone like this." Her smile was slight now, though real.

Oh, God, my heart.

She had no idea how *not* composed I'd been, time and again. I'd grieved her brother in Afghanistan, and by the time we got home, I'd cried my tears for him, for the most part. My focus had shifted to trying to keep Bec alive and figuring out how I could help her. So she'd never seen me. Only Ben and a few other soldiers had. I hadn't made a point to keep my mourning a secret. I wasn't afraid to cry. But I understood why Bec thought of me as always *composed*.

"That's really not true. You just haven't seen me." Grieving losing Dillon or, more recently, grieving losing her. Ben had seen some of that too, and clearly, he hadn't told her about it. I said a quick prayer of thanks for that.

"That may be so. I don't want you to think I'm enjoying your suffering. I do want to help. I brought some cold meds in case you didn't have any, a box of those super soft tissues, and a thermometer. Speaking of..." She hopped up and grabbed the little hand-held device, then swiped it over my forehead.

It beeped, and she flashed the screen at me, though I didn't see it.

"Looks normal."

I grunted.

She laughed.

"I repeat, you're mean."

She shook her head and tucked away another grin. "You're grumpy."

But then, she leaned close and smoothed a hand across my forehead and down to cradle my jaw. "I'm sorry you don't feel good, Thatcher. I wish I could make it better."

The touch and words were tender enough to cut through the fog, and my heart pulsed in response. Like it recognized how sweet she was being, even though she gave me a hard time.

"Thank you for coming."

Her hand dropped away and she stood.

"I'll get out of your space and let you rest. You better call me if you get worse and I'll come back." She gave me a stern look that said she meant business.

I nodded. "Will do. I'll be fine. Thank you."

Less than a minute later, she slipped out the door and I was alone again, the headache slightly better, and my whole body even feeling a little less weak. The inability to feed myself when I'd gotten home from rotation, and even more so, the empty fridge and cupboards, hadn't done me any favors. I was glad she'd brought me soup. Magical soup.

Magical Bec.

I tapped out a message. *"Thank you for coming. I wish I could've kissed you."*

Seconds later, she responded. *"Me too. Get better and then you can. At this point, I'll see you in Barcelona on Friday unless you need me to come back."*

I stared at the phone, absorbing the automatic consent to my kiss. I couldn't expend the mental energy to think through what that meant. The real implications. So, I settled on the couch. Hope, and Bec, and a trip to Spain were my happy companions as sleep pulled me under.

CHAPTER FIFTEEN

Bec

I hadn't seen Thatcher in six days.

I shouldn't have been missing him, checking my watch, practically ignoring my friends for him. No, I should not have. Yet somehow, he'd taken over my brain, and I couldn't pry him out. Though, to be honest, I hadn't tried very hard.

Because the man was... great. He was genuinely and completely great. Even his pathetic man-cold last weekend had been a legitimate cold. He'd still handled it like a man, of course. It was endearing and adorable right along with pathetic and ridiculous.

In fact, seeing him like that had filled me with a strange sense of nostalgia for years past when I'd taken care of Dillon. He was an utter baby about being sick—just helpless to the max. But I also got to take care of my brother, and at this stage, years later when I'd give anything to make him soup and brush the hair from his clammy forehead, thinking of a time when I had been able to do that was a strange kind of comfort.

Not that caring for Thatcher was anything like caring for Dillon. Obviously, there was never any attraction to my beloved, maddening brother. Thatcher, on the other hand… wow. I apparently found everything he did attractive. No, not suffering through his illness necessarily, but seeing him like that didn't totally turn me off, and that meant it was serious. That should be the test for proofing relationships— if you can care for a man when he's writhing in the agony of a stuffy nose and headache, then it's meant to be.

I tucked the smile away and sipped sangria, tuning back into Summer's story about a guy at the clinic. I was so glad she'd come with me and Emily. She was hilarious and bold in a sweet and charming way. I liked her. I wished I had a bit more of her sweetness in me. I'd long ago come to terms with the fact that I was kind of pushy and brash in a way that not everyone loved.

Thatcher seemed to like it well enough, even after everything. We had things to address if we wanted to move forward, but I couldn't wait for him to get here and just… enjoy being in Barcelona together.

It'd be hours, though. He and his friend couldn't find space on the same flight me and the girls had taken last night, so sadly, they were arriving late tonight and would head back with us on Sunday. That was okay. I'd take what-ever time I could, and I wouldn't let anything spoil my first effort to actually celebrate my birthday in years.

"The Sagrada Familia is just so immense. Beautiful and odd and special. Gaudi had such a vision." Summer sighed, then sipped her drink.

"It's stunning. And you're right, so unique compared to

other cathedrals. I think that's one of my favorite things about traveling Europe. You really come to love those structures and can make an entire day out of touring whatever version the city you're in has," Emily agreed.

We'd spent half a day walking to the part of the city that housed the cathedral, waited for our ticketed time to enter, and then toured, awe silencing us in the sacred, towering space. After that, we'd sat down for a lunchtime feast that'd taken nearly two hours, and then we'd taken naps.

So far, it'd been a perfect vacation day. Now we were having drinks before going to a paella cooking class. This had been Summer's suggestion, and Emily and I had both jumped on it. Before long, we were seated at a giant butcher-block table with eleven other people of all nationalities. The host, or chef, spoke in Spanish and English to talk through the course, and then we began.

First, we prepped fruit and mixed it with wine and sugar so we could drink Sangria later. Ultimately, the chef noted, the wine should sit with the ingredients much longer, but we could still enjoy it in a few hours.

Next, we measured out ingredients for *Crema Catalana*, the Spanish version of crème brûlée, and watched the process of simmering cinnamon and lemon in milk. After combining all the ingredients, we poured the liquid into clay pots, set them on trays, and put them in the large refrigerator to cool while we got to work on the paella.

We chopped vegetables—celery, leeks, even a turnip— and prepared other ingredients for the paella itself—beans, garlic, rice. Then we watched the chef guide us down a process I knew I'd never remember. I could cook decently well, though I didn't have a paella pan, and I didn't really do stuff that took this much time. Maybe because I only ever cooked for myself. Summer, however, watched with rapt attention to detail, studying the recipe and talking with the chef as she moved through each step in the process.

"Is she super into cooking?" I asked Emily quietly.

"I think it's her main hobby. She does a class like this wherever she goes, whenever she can. She also does feast nights, though I've never been able to attend. I think we need to get an invitation to dinner at her house, stat."

"I'm in."

The rest of the evening slipped by, and the much-awaited Sangria and paella were delightful. I'd never eaten anything as good as the paella, and I'd eaten it twice since coming to the city. It made me hope Summer's ability to recreate the dish would pan out so I could relive this meal in the months to come.

Then we had the *Crema Catalana*, and it tasted absolutely glorious. I loved cinnamon, so I knew I'd like it, but I didn't realize just how much. It. Was. Heaven. Creamy and flavorful without being heavy. The crunchy top we added with a torch just before refrigerating gave a nice crunch, even if my application ended up a bit heavy-handed and resulted in a more burnt-ish version than some.

By the end of the three-hour class, I felt sated and happy, and I'd managed to put Thatcher's impending arrival out of my head for most of it. Except for the persistent thoughts about him like, *I wonder if Thatcher likes Sangria? I wonder if Thatcher likes to cook? I wonder if Thatcher would take a class like this?*

Those inane questions reminded me how little I knew him now. I'd known him before, as well as one can know someone who one doesn't see in person very often. We'd poured our hearts out over the e-mails we shared for months. Until I'd stopped it.

Until I lost the ability to share myself.

And after that, he'd moved to the sidelines, my heart only able to care for itself and coddle its grief by ignoring it. Thatcher's behavior toward me had been kind and careful, and he and Ben had done everything they could to support me. I didn't let them do all that much, though, and if I needed a confidant, it'd been Erin, anyway. But all that time after I'd lost Dillon, I'd lost Thatcher, too.

I had years to catch up on, and more than that, I had simply so much more to learn about him. I didn't want to think about the wasted opportunities because I couldn't go back. We'd been reunited, and the more I sat with that reality, the more I felt sure I didn't want to waste this chance. Not again.

And what happens when he's injured, or worse, just like Dillon?

I slapped that thought away with every fiber of my being. I didn't need to think about nonsense like that right now. Not here, in Barcelona, on my happy birthday weekend.

When Thatcher texted that they'd landed, my heart leapt and giddiness filled me. Emily, Summer, and I had wandered the city slowly on the way back from the class. We delighted in the late-night atmosphere that came to life and would continue for hours even though it was already nearly eleven p.m.

We'd decided to head back to the apartment we were renting for the weekend and greet the boys. I didn't want to go out again, but if Thatcher wanted to, we could. Emily and Summer seemed interested in going dancing. I, however, was dragging a bit. I hadn't slept much the night before because my stupid brain couldn't shut down with all the anticipation of the weekend.

What felt like hours, though was not even a full hour

later, a buzz interrupted our laughter, and the resident butterflies in my belly took flight. *He's here!*

I sprang to my feet and ran to the door, threw it open—and the sight of a man I didn't know, who looked vaguely familiar, greeted me.

"Uh, hi."

A twitch of a nice pair of lips and then he said, "Hi. I'm Rob Waverly. Thatcher's friend. He's still on the street trying to extricate himself from a conversation with the cabbie."

"Is everything okay?" Dumbly, I attempted to glance behind him and found I couldn't see past his bulky arms and shoulders.

The man's mouth turned up in a half-smile. "You know Thatcher, right? You're his girl?"

My stomach dropped. "Uh—"

"So you know how he is. Too nice. He speaks just enough Spanish to make the guy think he could truly understand him. Guy got talking about his grandkids, and now Thatch's getting a full family history complete with photos."

"I'm here, I'm here. He finally let me go," came Thatcher's voice.

Again, Rob basically blocked out the entire doorway so I couldn't see.

"Come on in," I said to Rob, urgency building inside me. I needed to set eyes on Thatcher.

Rob shuffled past, and in retrospect, I could hear voices —likely him introducing himself to Summer and Emily. I quite literally only had eyes, ears, and attention for Thatcher.

He gripped one strap of a backpack over his shoulder, but he let his bag slip to the floor before he held out his arms and I jumped into them. I hadn't planned to greet him like this. But the emotional and physical momentum made it feel like being close to him, seeing him in person and feeling that he was really there, had become a biological imperative.

"I'm so glad you're here." I shut my eyes and breathed him in—the warmth of his skin and the scent of his laundry with a little lingering stale eau de airplane.

He smiled against my cheek. "Me too. Finally."

"I'm sorry you got delayed." I pulled back, my eyes ravenous for his face, even after less than a week. Had it really only been six days? Maybe I was making up for the years and years of lost time.

"I'm just glad we made it today. I didn't want to miss your actual birthday." He smiled sweetly, then took in my shirt and jeans, and his eyes darkened before they returned to meet mine again. "You look good."

"You do too." He did. He always did. He always had, and the first time I saw him, I'd thought, *That's him.* Some part of me echoed that back every time now, even still. "Come in. Let's get your stuff settled and then we can figure out if we want to do something tonight."

His eyes widened. "Okay."

I laughed. "Are you still an *early to bed* kind of guy?"

"I am."

I leaned close. "Don't worry. You couldn't pay me to go back out. I think those three might be planning to, though."

From the looks of it, Summer, Emily, and Rob were gearing up to head out for the evening. They would have to go without me. I liked a late night here or there, though not as much as I used to. We'd already planned on a long day tomorrow, and I didn't want to be dragging around Barcelona on my birthday. I wanted to feel good, look good, and simply celebrate.

I showed Thatcher the room he and Rob would share

and then broke the news to Emily and Summer. They cracked jokes about how I planned to take advantage of Thatcher with them gone, but ultimately, they understood. They promised to be quiet when they came in and then left, chatting happily with Rob on the way out.

The door shut behind them, and the apartment fell quiet.

"Wow. Rob's up for anything, isn't he?" I commented, willing myself to stay calm. We'd been alone often enough before. It shouldn't have made me feel winded.

Thatcher raised a brow where he sat on the couch. "He's outgoing, friendly. He's on a super strict training program so he's unlikely to drink, but the dude loves to go out and dance, especially with beautiful women."

I narrowed my eyes just slightly. It was nice he was calling my friends beautiful. Sadly, the ugly, selfish part of me wanted him not to notice. I wasn't proud to admit it, but *I* wanted to be beautiful to him, and a lame, selfish part of me wanted to be the only one.

He chuckled. "Yes, you know your friends are beautiful. Obviously, you fit right in with them."

I delivered a glass of water to the table next to him, then sat so my knees angled toward him on the couch. "They are. Emily's got that polished, corporate look that is totally at odds with how down-to-earth she is, and Summer... I mean, you're right. She's exceptionally pretty."

They both were, really. And I liked that Thatcher acknowledged it. What would be the point of pretending other beautiful people didn't exist, anyway? That first shot of jealousy at his recognition had fizzled, mostly because Thatcher didn't play games. He didn't ever act interested in someone else when we were together. More than that, I'd never been someone who needed to be the only pretty girl in the room, and I enjoyed my gorgeous friends. They were beautiful in every way, and I felt glad Thatcher was a man who could recognize that right along with me.

For that matter... "Your friend Rob is, uh, quite impressive."

Thatcher nearly spit out his water but swallowed it down before speaking. "Don't *ever* let him hear you say that. Dude has an ego the size of Alaska. He's a beast. A guy at work is training him up for—uh, well, he's training him, and so he's becoming more and more of a machine."

"He's training for an Army thing?"

"Yeah, just trying to get into a different job, and fitness is part of the new job description. Masters is looking to retire in the next few years, and no doubt he'll move into training people full time." He set his water down, then dropped his hand to rest on my knee.

My insides flipped.

"Masters is in the Army, but he's training this guy—is that his job in the Army?" My brain moved slowly, only properly processing Thatcher's nearness and circling the touch on my knee. All other information didn't seem to penetrate the haze.

Thatcher patted my knee, then turned his palm up and waited. My heart skipped, but I set my hand in his. He laced our fingers together and smiled.

"He's a sergeant first class in the infantry. If you think Rob seems like a beast, Masters is the ultimate. I don't know. He's an odd duck and excellent at what he does. In fact, he came to the fest last month but left early."

"Oh!" I exclaimed before I could stop myself. "The Adonis!"

He gave me a shocked look. "Seriously?"

I held up both hands. "Hey, you're the one who called him that."

He stewed a moment, squinty eyes showing me his fake displeasure. "True."

I watched, enjoying the little flare of jealousy he showed me now and remembering the last time this Masters guy had come up. Thatcher had asked about my type, and I didn't get to tell him. Maybe I should now.

"I see what you're saying. I didn't really get a good look at him, but he did strike me as rather fit." I pressed my lips together, knowing the understatement was ridiculous since the man looked like he ate barbells for breakfast. He wasn't obnoxiously big. He had a neck, and he didn't look 'roided out or anything. Still, basically everything about him said, *I am incredibly strong, fit, and attractive. My progeny will survive.*

Then you looked at his face and it had this stoic, almost harsh kind of beauty. I didn't see him smile once, and he'd been sitting by Emily—who was extremely funny and likable—which probably meant he had no sense of humor. Also a thumbs down for the man.

"Yeah. *Rather fit.* The man is ridiculous, but I'm done talking about him. I want to talk about you. How was your day? How was your cooking class?"

And with that, I filled him in on every detail of our day. We talked and talked, slowly moving closer together and finding reasons to touch each other. Though part of me felt desperate to kiss him, we didn't start anything like that, somehow both sensing we should wait.

I didn't know what time we dozed off. When I woke in the night, I didn't bother moving to my bed. I didn't want to miss a moment with Thatcher. Not another moment.

CHAPTER SIXTEEN

Thatcher

We spent the day in a group for the most part. We visited the famous Boqueria market that had every kind of fresh food you could imagine, where we also ate lunch, and then we wandered around the Gothic Quarter. After lunch, we'd split since the girls wanted to shop, and Rob and I went to explore some military sights. When we got back, the girls were napping, and I felt the lost opportunity acutely.

Because that morning, I'd awoken to Bec's head on my chest and her arm over my torso. My back had been aching, and I'd overheated from being plastered together on the small couch, but I hadn't moved. I'd kept my breathing calm and closed my eyes so I could absorb the feel of her body against mine.

I didn't remember falling asleep, but I was glad we had. Otherwise, I would've dragged myself to my room and she would have gone to hers, and we wouldn't have had that time together. Even if we had been asleep, I felt grateful for it.

Those quiet moments before anyone else woke had belonged to me and me alone. I'd braced for the bitterness and resentment to flood in to remind me that this woman had left me and still kept me at arm's length, but it never came.

I'd lain there, her head rising and falling with my breath, and thanked God for her. I wanted to only feel grateful for her, especially today. I'd thought of Dillon then and thanked God for him too. He was a good man, and because of him, I'd known and loved Bec.

Where we went from here, I couldn't tell. My heart had clenched, almost to the point of hurting, for how much I wanted more mornings like this, wrapped up in her. I wanted her trust—her abandon. And just as she started to shift and wake, I'd vowed to do whatever I could to see this through.

She'd stirred, then dragged a hand over her face and squinted up at me with one eye. Then she'd held a hand over her mouth and said, "I wish I was one of those dainty women who could fall asleep with contacts in and makeup on and wake up looking beautiful, but... this is real life. So I'll be right back."

She'd shuffled to the bathroom, and I'd chuckled, my heart warm and glad, embracing the truth. I loved her. I'd never stopped. And, if anything, that love had grown and multiplied. Our time apart hadn't stopped it or crushed it or removed it. It had paused, waiting.

Much to my disappointment, Rob had stumbled out of our room before Bec had finished in the bathroom and begun his report of the night before. Soon enough, all of us were sitting around the table sipping coffee, searching for what we wanted to do on our phones.

Bec had shot me a few looks that had filled me up with anticipation and longing, but clearly, we wouldn't have another minute alone for a while.

And hours later, when she stepped out of the room in a dark green dress, her hair in loose waves down to her shoulders, golden heels making her at least three inches taller, I lost my breath. I could hear Emily and Summer in the bathroom, and Rob paced in our room while making a call. This would be our minute alone.

I hopped up and moved to her, gazing down at her beautiful face. I should've set things up better—should've finagled time alone with privacy. Sadly, I hadn't, and she'd wanted everyone together anyway. But I wouldn't wait any longer.

"Happy birthday, Bec."

She smiled, genuine and open. "Thank you. I'm glad you're here."

"I am too." I took her hands in mine and pushed down a jump of nerves. "I have something for you. It's small, but I think it's a good time to give it to you."

Her brows raised. "You didn't have to get me anything. Just coming on this trip is more than enough."

"I know." I handed her a small, blue velvet bag cinched closed.

She opened it and pulled the material so the silver-dollar-sized coin dropped out.

"It's a commander's coin. Different military leadership has them to give to people when they visit, or when someone does something notable. It's an old military custom that has persisted—boosts morale."

She studied it, flipping it to the opposite side to read the inscription.

"This one was Dillon's. He'd gotten it for helping a general with something. I found it after everything happened, and I kept it. But it's time to pass it on to you."

She licked her lips and her eyes shined, but she swallowed past the tears. "Thank you. It's good to have a little piece of something that was his from that time."

I shook my head, amazed. "Of course."

She smiled, and my heart kicked, wanting to tell her so much. But I settled for a few immediate thoughts. "You're so beautiful, Bec. I love your humor. How you care for your friends. I love how you've honored Dillon's memory with this trip, and with getting to a place where you could enjoy it. He'd be proud of you."

She blinked, then swallowed again.

"I know. He would be." She pressed her lips together, steadying herself, then spoke. "I'm so happy you could be with me this year on this day. It makes it better to have you with me because you knew him, and how great he was, and you know how far I've come."

I didn't... not completely anyway. But I did know she was so different from the woman who could barely speak her brother's name, who couldn't stand to be near anyone who'd known him on her birthday, much less *celebrate* it.

"You're amazing," I said, a little breathless and feeling awed by her strength.

She beamed. "You are too."

I searched her eyes, the pull toward her irresistible. I leaned down just as she looped her hands over my shoulders, and I kissed her. Hunger and relief swept through me as I took her mouth with mine, tasting and claiming in a kiss far more passionate than we'd shared thus far.

The sounds of a door opening caused us both to separate enough to break the kiss, but I didn't let her go, and she didn't release me either.

"Oh, hello. Sorry to interrupt," Rob said cheerily.

"No, you're not," I said, not looking away from Bec's deep blue eyes.

"Well, *I* am. But we do have to get to dinner if we're going to get a good spot at the bar for dancing after," Emily said from behind Bec.

Summer said something else. I couldn't have guessed what, because rather than moving away, Bec pressed against me, bringing us even closer than before. My stomach dropped, and I instinctively pulled her to me with my hands on her lower back.

"We'll be right there. You guys go ahead." Her voice came out steady and normal, but it left no room to question her.

I loved that about her. It could be maddening at times because it meant that arguing with her was like arguing with a brick wall. That characterized the last few interactions we'd had before she'd left Tennessee. She knew her mind. And I couldn't be happier that, in this instant, she knew she wanted another moment alone with me.

The door of the rented apartment clicked shut, and she urged me back down. Her tongue swept in, and this time, she controlled the kiss. My heart threatened to beat out of my chest as her fingers caressed my neck.

With a regretful moan, she ended the kiss and stepped back. "That should tide me over."

"Tide you over until when?"

Her eyes sparkled before she turned and opened the door. "Until the next time you kiss me. Which I hope will be at least once an hour for the rest of the day. That's another gift you can give me."

I grabbed her hand and pulled her with me to the stairs. "I would be happy to oblige."

We feasted on a dinner I'd remember for a long time. The girls had found some famous tapas place, and we'd eaten and eaten and eaten. Literally *hours* of eating. The great thing was, the small, flavorful dishes shared between us didn't fill us up. By the end, of course we were all full of great food and wine, and the process of eating had been part of the evening's events.

After the main meal, they brought out a giant cake, and we'd cheered for Bec, though we'd refrained from singing happy birthday like idiots, which she clearly appreciated.

Then we moved to a club that I would've assumed targeted Americans since it'd been named after an American president. A sliver of disappointment wormed its way in when Emily mentioned this fact. But once we arrived, we were clearly the minority, if not some of the only Americans. I didn't mind seeing my fellow countrymen, though I did wonder at the logic of traveling somewhere if you didn't explore the new things another culture had to offer.

People packed the place, but they'd reserved a section of tables with a great view of the microphone where a man with a guitar had set up.

"This guy is incredible. I hope you're going to dance with us, Thatcher."

Emily smiled at me, and I nodded gamely. Apparently, she, Summer, and Rob had come last night and danced until three in the morning. They'd asked if he was playing anywhere tonight, and as luck had it, he planned to play the same place again.

"I'm not sure I knew you dance." Bec bit her lip, and her eyes slid over me like the idea of me dancing did things to her.

"I'm not sure you'd have a reason to. And, yeah, I'll dance with you, birthday girl."

Her smile blazed, and then she stood and reached across the tiny table to pull me over it. I leaned in, and she pressed a kiss to my lips before pushing me away and plopping back in her seat. I laughed and shook my head at her like I thought she was crazy, mostly so I wouldn't betray my real thoughts. Thoughts like, *You should always do that* or *You can have whatever you want from me* or *I love you and I never want to be without you.*

Those were not thoughts to share on a night when we'd all had a lot of wine and we were in a big group on a birthday trip. Those were back home, alone, quiet conversation things to share.

A waitress took drink orders, and the first song started. It took only minutes before the space in front of the musician flooded with bodies and it didn't stop. The guy took one ten-minute break. Other than drink breaks and a trip into the bowels of the building for a pit stop, we danced the rest of the night.

We all danced full out, too. Everyone did. Bodies jumping and twirling and generally just enjoying the great music played by a talented person. He played current hits from the radio and some amazing Spanish music we didn't know, but that didn't keep us from dancing. I hadn't danced this much since my sister's wedding, and that'd been nearly a decade now.

We left when the music man did, just after three a.m.

By the time we reached the apartment, we were happily exhausted. One small peck to Bec's lips was all I got for a good night, and then the day, the trip, came to an end.

I lay waiting for sleep, Rob already passed out in the neighboring bed, and sifted through the snapshots of the evening. Bec's eyes on mine. Bec's body nested with mine, rocking to the music. Her hands all over me and mine on her. Man, it'd been hot all night. Literally hot and *stifling* in other ways, especially considering I needed absolutely no help wanting her. Eventually though, I eased away from those musings, knowing they wouldn't help me settle down, and finally fell asleep.

The next morning, we rushed through packing and sped to the airport to catch our midday flight that felt early since we'd stayed out so late. It had to be the minimal sleep and too much wine and hours on my feet. As the plane took off back to Munich, I couldn't help feeling a sense that I was leaving behind something good, and nothing in front of me would ever match it.

CHAPTER SEVENTEEN

Bec

Summer, Emily, and I got to sit together on the way home. Thatcher and Rob were each in different parts of the cramped plane since they'd booked later.

I didn't want it to be over. Returning to normal life at Kugelfels made me feel unaccountably sad. I wasn't normally like this. I liked going home and gearing up for whatever next trip I had planned, or even planning the next adventure. But I did like having a home base.

Years ago, when I traveled more weekends than not with my aunt, I hated going home to the empty apartment I should've shared with Dillon. I also hated being home. I hated so much about life then, I just did whatever seemed remotely right.

Remembering the tangled emotions that accompanied travel and returning home back then, I silently said a prayer of thanks for how I'd grown. I missed Dillon, and there'd been times, especially yesterday, where that missing winded me. It'd been six years since we'd celebrated a birthday together, and a little under five since he'd passed.

Having Thatcher there... it hadn't made it harder. It'd made the experience of celebrating the gift of life so much richer. I wished more than once during the day that I'd been able to see it that way years ago, and that I hadn't run from the sadness and fear. Those emotions had followed me right to Germany, and by the time I'd arrived, I couldn't avoid addressing them.

In truth, I'd had to leave. The people in Tennessee had loved me, but they'd allowed me to avoid the grief. Or, maybe I'd fooled them all into believing I processed it in my own way rather than blocking it out completely.

But now... now I wanted days like yesterday. I wanted that complex weave of new experience twining with the weft of heavy emotions and memory. Thatcher knew Dillon, and he knew me before and through some of the darkest days of my life. It wasn't just that he *had* known me. He was fun and so full of joy, and his perspective and ability to open himself to new experiences made him an amazing travel companion. And I wanted him to know me now, even better than he was starting to.

As the plane touched down in Munich, I wished for another day together, just the two of us, in the magic that was the city of Barcelona. Looking ahead, we needed time alone, and I ultimately had to address the depth of my feelings and the pain I'd caused him. We hadn't broached the subject of my fleeing Tennessee since our first few interactions, and that wasn't fair.

So, as we made our way through the airport to the exits, I grabbed his hand. "Can you come over for dinner on Tuesday?"

He smiled down and laced our fingers together. "I'd love to. What can I bring?"

~

Monday morning dragged in like a half-drowned cat. The soldiers all had the day off, while the schools, Ed Center, and most on-post offices were still open. Usually, that'd mean we'd have a decent number of service members coming in to talk about school or testing or whatever, but the clock clutched at the minutes like a miser with his gold.

I may have woken up feeling dramatic. After sitting alone in my office, no e-mails to respond to and no meetings on my schedule, I had to get out. I wandered out into the lobby area and leaned against the admin desk.

"How are you settling in, Katie?"

She'd been with us a few weeks and was completely over-qualified, like so many of the military spouses who took jobs on post.

She looked up from the open book on her desk and smiled. "I'm good. Noah was confused by my having to work today, which was funny. Otherwise, it's good."

"Well, I'm with him. We should be closed since I bet you not a single soldier walks through that door today, but we'll see."

Emily swept in the front doors then, looking thoroughly hassled. "I hate my car."

"No, you don't. You love that thing," I countered because she frequently mentioned her devotion to her BMW.

"Well, today I hate it."

It'd broken down on her, though luckily the dealership had given her a loaner while they dealt with whatever issue needed fixing. All of that took several hours, so she'd missed the two slowest hours of the day. Well, not including the last hour, which usually multiplied into exponential swaths of time untethered to any real, temporal measure, and often served to drive everyone working into a sense of end-of-day madness.

She scuttled down the hall balancing her purse, a messenger bag, a giant water bottle, and a huge coffee thermos. Seconds later, she came to stand next to me and checked my hip with hers, so I scooted over.

"I think we should all go out this weekend. Your husband is on rotation, right Katie?"

Katie perked up. "He is. I want to go into Regensburg for dinner and wander around. I already asked a couple of women I met. Maybe we could all go together?"

"Fun! I'll ask Summer. We can see if Donna or anyone else wants to come too." Emily slapped the countertop, then pushed away, seemingly energized to have plans. "Better go check e-mail and all that jazz."

Katie and I watched her go, then smiled at each other. Emily was truly a character.

"Are your friends other Army spouses?" I asked, not eager to return to my lonely office.

"One is. Livie Anderson? Or, I guess, maybe Wolfe? I'm not sure. She and Colonel Wolfe got married this past summer. He's the battalion commander of the OPFOR. And then her sister-in-law, Ariel Wolfe? She's here as the colonel's nanny."

"Wow. Isn't that your husband's boss?" And come to think of it, it'd be Thatcher's boss too.

She chuckled and her cheeks heated. "Yes. I actually got to know him a little bit while Noah was missing. And when I first moved out here, Livie basically attached herself to me to show me around and help me get acclimated. With that, I met Ariel and a few of Livie's teacher friends. It has definitely helped, because honestly, Noah didn't hang out with many married soldiers, so his friends are mostly just other single soldiers."

"Ah, yeah. I can see how that could make getting to know people extra tricky. I'm glad Livie took you under her wing." She sounded like a nice person. I looked forward to meeting her.

A thought flashed through my mind. I wondered if I should tell Thatcher I planned to hang out with his boss's wife. Probably not. It seemed like people mixed and mingled here more than they did on larger posts. And plus, I wasn't Thatcher's... anything.

It hit me then. We hadn't had any conversation about what we were doing. It felt like we were together, though we hadn't exactly relaxed into a relationship. I guess I had one more thing I needed to bring up at dinner tomorrow.

My belly fluttered. I pushed that away and focused on Katie, who'd been speaking.

"What time do you think? Should we try to get the train together or just meet out there?"

From that point, we talked through all the details, and then I left her to her book, happy to focus on the weekend plans instead of my nerves over dinner with Thatcher.

All the nervous energy that'd been buzzing around me could go ahead and take a flying leap because Thatcher canceled on me. Granted, he had a really good reason, but still. As a company commander, he was in charge of everyone in his company, more than a hundred soldiers, and when crazy crap happened, he and his first sergeant were on the hook to deal with it. One of his soldiers had been rushed to the hospital late in the day and another had some drama with housing.

I didn't know the people, and it was hard to summon compassion for situations I didn't really know anything about, except that they took Thatcher away from me. I tried not to begrudge them, even if I didn't understand the urgency. This was a good reminder of the reality of his work and how it broke into his regular life, too. But that, as always, I didn't want to think about. So I locked *those* thoughts away.

I'd been mentally preparing for our evening together since we'd deplaned on Sunday, and the days since had stretched out, long and thin, just to spite me. I couldn't continue to moan or whine or be an unempathetic sociopath, so I took a deep breath, ate my homemade lasagna alone, and toasted to the empty apartment.

Also, I researched places for dinner on Friday and worked to channel my restlessness toward that activity. I would enjoy getting to know some new faces since, thus far, outside of work, I knew Emily, Summer, Thatcher, Rob, and now Katie. I'd been here too long to only have a few friends, and that wouldn't do me any favors in the long run.

I needed to set down some roots here. Make friends and invest in life. I'd never really done that at Stuttgart, primarily because after working through the counseling sessions, I didn't want to stay there forever. I was grateful for it, and that would never change, but I'd needed a fresh start.

Kugelfels presented an interesting conundrum in that regard. I'd come for a new leaf, and I'd joined an old boss. I'd come for a second chance, or third maybe, and yet I'd ended up reuniting with a man who embodied my *first* chance—the only chance I'd ever really wanted to take, but felt I couldn't.

Where did that leave me? Old and new mixed and mingled, and I didn't quite know what to do about it. For the first time in months, I felt the twinge to run. Like maybe this was all a big mistake and rather than making different plans with Thatcher and going out with girlfriends, I should run far and fast and save myself the inevitable hurt.

CHAPTER EIGHTEEN

Thatcher

Major Nate Reynolds didn't wear his perma-grin like he usually did. *Not a good sign.*

I'd seen his serious side only once before, right after I'd encountered Bec for the first time and she'd refused to even catch up. It'd sent me to a fairly dark, self-pitying place, I could admit now in retrospect. I hadn't anticipated that—how could I? I didn't expect to walk into the Ed Center and see Bec after years. I certainly didn't expect her to essentially tell me she didn't want anything to do with me.

Granted, that was stupid because hadn't she told me just that by ignoring me, refusing to communicate, and leaving without a goodbye?

I cleared away those thoughts, as they wouldn't help me now. The last few days had been insane—maybe it was the full moon or the angst of the upcoming rotations that would take us, except for Thanksgiving, right up until winter break.

"I asked you four here because I'm looking for answers. Colonel Wolfe's away, so that's one possible explanation, though I don't think it's that simple. Something's broken here, and we need to figure out how we might fix it."

Major Reynolds folded his hands together and leaned his forearms on his desk. We were meeting in the conference room since he didn't have an office big enough for four people, and we needed confidentiality for this discussion.

"People get crazy when rotations are back-to-back like this. That's all it is," Rob Waverly submitted. Though, guaranteed, we'd all been thinking it.

"Yeah, well, I'm sitting here looking at Serious Incident Reports for two DWIs, a domestic separation due to violence, a sexual harassment complaint, two soldiers hospitalized for different reasons, and a small handful of other nonsense I don't even know how to classify." Major Reynolds' frown deepened, and he mumbled something under his breath.

"Sir, most of this is just happenstance. Purely coincidental it's all hitting now. That said, I do think Waverly's right—tensions are high right now. They've been working nonstop since block leave other than, what, three weekends? That's nearly four months of work with very little time to blow off steam. This can't be all that big of a surprise." Mick Farrell had a way of putting things plainly, even talking to leadership, that I didn't. He always got the message across.

Major Reynolds didn't seem pleased. "Well, great. We'll time-travel back a year and tell the planners this isn't going to work because the soldiers won't feel like doing their jobs every day. They'll only want to do them some days."

Whoa. Reynolds was *not* happy. All four of us captains

sat straighter in our seats, though I didn't know how it was possible. Not typical of the major, for sure.

"Point taken, sir," I said, because I'd learned the hard way that not responding when leadership spoke wasn't wise. Granted, sometimes people wanted to just muse aloud with an audience, so then you had to know and just stay quiet. Fortunately for all of us, Reynolds, and LTC Wolfe, for that matter, weren't big monologuers. They wanted input from their leaders, and I respected that.

Reynolds didn't speak, and the other three captains shifted in their seats. I had only a few suggestions, none of which were gold, but I waded in. "I have a few ideas, sir, if you're up for hearing them."

The major waved me on without a word, and I dove in.

The rotation would start in less than eight hours. I had to be in early, and I needed as much sleep as I could get before then. But more than all that, I had to see Bec. I'd canceled our dinner thanks to the soldiers's shenanigans, and we had so much unresolved. We wouldn't be diving into any of that tonight, but I'd texted to ask her if I could swing by on the way home, and she'd said yes.

Part of me feared she'd say no. Or just not respond. I recognized that fear for what it was—a lack of trust. The aftereffects of her shutting me out and moving across the world still hung heavily around my heart at times, and I couldn't just make that disappear. Yet, I wanted to trust her, and I genuinely wanted that looming sense of... *something...* to go away.

I knocked on her door and she threw it open, then

reached for my uniform and pulled me inside by a handful of the top.

"I missed you," she said in a rush, then hugged me so tightly, she knocked the air out of me.

I held her close, dipping my head to breathe in her sweet shampoo and savor this moment of simple pleasure. Times like these sent doubts and mistrust to the moon.

We embraced for minutes, not seconds, each of us taking comfort in simply being close. I hadn't realized how much I needed this. As she released me and looked up with an almost timid look, my heart pinched.

"What?" I asked, because *that* was not a Bec Jones look.

"What do you mean?" Her head tipped to the side in question, then she turned and paced away.

"You just gave me a look I don't think I've ever seen on you. It looked... *shy*."

She busied herself in the kitchen pouring glasses of water, then returned and handed me one. We stayed standing by the bar-top of her counter.

"I've been a little unsure about what's going on with us. And I don't like that." Her deep blue eyes circled around my face, then returned to meet my gaze.

I couldn't hide my smile. That was the Bec I knew—a bit grumpy about feeling unsure, but still willing to say it. It was an odd dichotomy—she could be blunt and up front, then ran away from anything really difficult.

Had run away. That was in the past. And it sounded like she hadn't kept running. She'd faced her fear and grief when she'd landed.

She kept running from you.

The thought sliced through, sobering me.

"You want to talk about this right now?" It came out edged with a harshness I didn't recognize, and I couldn't take it back. My mood had swung from one end of feeling—joyful and relieved—to the other.

Her brow dropped low, and she licked her lips before speaking. "Uh, I guess not? I thought you had a rotation coming up, and I figured it'd be better to just... touch base now? But I'm sure you need to get home and rest up."

I hated the way this conversation was playing out, though I couldn't figure out how to stop it. Other than to be open and tell her what I needed. Not just from her, but generally, right now. I let out a sigh that sounded more tired than frustrated.

"I'm sorry. I'm exhausted, and it's been a crap week. I wanted to see you—*had* to see you—before I go into the next few weeks. I'm sorry I missed our date. I don't like going days without seeing you." I set my hands on her shoulders and looked down at her.

Her brow had cleared, and though she wasn't smiling, her expression had eased.

She took a breath. "I know it's silly and we have a lot of other stuff to discuss, but are we... dating? Exclusively?"

A laugh burst out of me. "You think I'm about to date someone else?"

Her lips pressed together, but I could see a hint of a smile at the corner.

"Are you?"

"Are *you*?" I inched closer, crowding her.

She chuckled. "Definitely not."

"Same for me."

"Good."

"Yeah. Good."

She bit her lip, which contained her smile a bit.

I grinned. "We have a lot more to talk about. I hate to keep saying that and putting it off, but I don't want to have those conversations now. I want to kiss you for a few minutes, now that you're officially my girlfriend, and then I have to go."

My hands landed on either side of her waist, and she rose to the tips of her toes and wrapped her arms around my neck. The kiss held all the urgency and longing that'd built up over the week. Even a hint of panic around the edges. Need to be close, to press her to me, keep her by me, make her want me the way I wanted her.

Make her love me.

My hands slid around to her lower back, then smoothed down over her perfect curves to the backs of her legs and pulled just as she hopped. I moved, the kiss still blazing, her legs wrapped around my waist, and dropped onto the couch, our lips parting for only the moment of impact.

She pressed closer, her hands sliding over my arms and then mapping my chest. My breath caught as they continued down, down between us, then stopped. Waiting.

No real thought came to me. Thankfully, my body responded in a miraculously logical way, which didn't even make sense, but I had to roll with it. I broke the kiss and hugged her close, then leaned away so I could see her. Her eyes were fire and wanting, and I shuddered with energy and the same desire I saw there.

"Sorry. I'm sorry," she said, breathless and blushing and so *so* beautiful.

"No. No. No apologies. Just not..." Oh, good Lord, everything hurt. The slightly embarrassed look on her face, the way she pulled away and stood to the side. My body. My heart. *Damn.*

"Just not..." she repeated, waiting.

I stood and rubbed a hand across my chin, then took her hand. "Yet. Just not yet."

She nodded.

I walked to the door, her hand in mine. "Thank you for seeing me tonight."

"Thanks for coming."

We kissed—just a quick farewell—then I left, dragging a sack of frustration, desire, anticipation, and dread behind me.

CHAPTER NINETEEN

Bec

The train rattled along, barreling toward a girls' night I felt patently *not* up for. But I would show up and buck the hell up and stop moping.

I hadn't managed that since Thatcher had left last night. The door shut and I had dumped out his water, set the glass in the sink, and slunk off to get ready for bed feeling a mixture of embarrassment, frustration, and oddly, defeat.

Not that I'd set out to *win* something, though if I was honest, I couldn't help feeling let down by our interaction. And truly, not because I'd been ready to move things to another level and he'd backed off. I'd lost my head there for a minute, which I can't really even blame myself for because the whole *hike me up around his waist and carry me to the couch* thing had thrown me for a delicious kind of loop.

His slowing us down was wise, and honestly, not a surprise. I only felt bad that he might've felt pressured or like I didn't respect his boundaries. Then, there came more frustration because what *were* his boundaries? What did he want, and what wasn't on the table? We hadn't had any of those conversations, and we needed to.

Last night wasn't the night. He'd had an awful week, and he had to start work early. He'd already warned me he could only come by for a few minutes. We needed time. How had we not found time in Spain? How could I go another two weeks until we talked? The rotation would be nearly non-stop for him until early November, and after that, he literally had one weekend off and then it started again. The soldiers here had to be exhausted.

My chest hollowed out at the thought. *Soldiers.* I breathed through the flood of nonsensical, pure fear that shook my hands. I could sit and think about that, about Thatcher and rotations and him being a soldier, or I could think more about last night. I could remember his strength, the curve of his cheek under my palm, the heat of his mouth. And I could shove those other thoughts away, down into a dark corner where I didn't have to look at them.

That's better. Way better. Keep going on like that.

I missed him. It was stupid to say it now, when I was getting to see him so often, yet since I'd opened myself to feelings for him, I couldn't shut them off. They had no place to go when I didn't get to see him. Not that I needed to be able to love him *physically*, but we hadn't resolved all the distance between us, still.

Still.

I could hardly stand knowing he had things to say, and so did I, and yet we hadn't just *said them*. It drove me up the wall, and then in person, I grew nervous or feared the time wasn't right.

I exhaled and sifted in my purse for my lip gloss. As I

swiped it on, I thought of Thatcher's lips on mine. His hands on me. Oh, goodness, I liked all of it.

And I couldn't bemoan everything that'd happened the night before—not by a long shot. Though the dynamic of the conversation had been odd, to say the least, we'd clarified we were officially together. For someone who'd run from the man years ago and who hadn't had a relationship since before I met him, the status of *girlfriend* was momentous.

The train screeched to a halt and I hopped out, then shuffled along with the crowd up the stairs, along the raised walkway, down the escalators, and finally out onto the street. At just after six p.m., the daylight was waning. The days were getting shorter. I needed to think of a plan for the holidays, or soon it'd be too late. Since Kugelfels was so small and basically everyone had leave over the winter break, I'd heard it became a ghost town. If I didn't want to stick around for that, I should travel. That said, the Ed Center, bizarrely, was still open quite a few of the days surrounding the holidays. So I could work, though rumor had it no one came in between Christmas and New Year's.

I tucked my coat tighter around me and hunched into a particularly cold gust. I'd figure out the winter break thing soon. Maybe we'd even talk about plans at dinner tonight and I could get some ideas.

I rounded the corner into a small courtyard surrounded by high stone walls—I'd turned my phone's GPS on silent, though I definitely needed it since I didn't know my way around Regensburg very well just yet. One minute I'd been walking on a regular, if ancient-feeling street, gazing at the spires of a gorgeous cathedral. And the next, I'd ducked through a stone archway in a wall on the path and now stood, transported to another little world.

The cobblestones were crisp and clean—not unlike most of Germany, from my experience thus far. In front of me bloomed a glorious garden that seemed to sprout out of the rocks in the street. On closer inspection, it was a small, gated plot with raised beds about ten feet by ten. A blossoming tree and other cold-hardy wildflowers sprung out around it in yellows, oranges, purples, and reds.

I chuckled to myself and stopped, momentarily stuck in place by the beautiful surprise of the space. I loved that about traveling around and living in Europe. These cities, established hundreds of years before any city in the US, always held magical little secrets like this. Discovering them made them feel like *mine*. They then felt familiar and more like home.

And just like that, Regensburg became a little bit mine. I breathed in, eyes shut, and let the feeling wash over me another moment, then pulled open the door to the restaurant.

After everyone arrived and introductions were made, we ordered drinks while sitting at a secluded corner table and all became fast friends. Livie Anderson-Wolfe was delightful—warm and welcoming and open, and she'd worked on Kugelfels for more than three years. Her sister-in-law, Ariel Wolfe, was shy, though she seemed to be warming up as the evening wore on. She was apparently celebrating her one-year anniversary at Kugelfels, though I got the feeling she was uneasy about that, but I couldn't tell why.

And Katie Miller was adorable and sweet, and way too freaking smart to be the admin at the Ed Center. Apparently, she was working on her master's in education administration through Duke online... so, a real dummy. We tried to keep our Ed Center talk to a minimum for Livie's and Ariel's sakes, but they were tuned in enough to the soldiers, and I guessed Livie's husband's work, that they were interested in some of the issues we mentioned.

Summer sat quietly for the most part, especially when the food came. I'd noticed this about her—all her attention became absorbed by the food when eating. I realized, belatedly, she was the only one not in education in some way or another. She didn't seem to mind based on the dreamy look she wore after each bite of her dinner.

"Bec, did I hear correctly that you're with Thatcher Wild?" Livie asked before taking a drink of her wine.

My stomach flipped at the mention of Thatcher—of being *with* him like we were an item. But we were. I wondered where she'd heard that because I hadn't mentioned it.

"Yes, I am." I smiled, then took a bite of my schnitzel since I had no idea what else to say.

"Eric thinks the world of him. He's mentioned several times what an excellent officer he is and how he knows he's going far in the Army."

"That's always good to hear," I said, unsure how to accept accolades for my boyfriend. Not a thing I'd ever gotten even close to doing before.

"Noah respects him too. He was always really kind to me—from the moment I met him. You're a lucky woman," Katie added.

"Oh, *Thatcher Wild*. I have heard both Eric and Nate mention him in very positive terms. That's so great." Ariel smiled.

"Is Nate your partner?" I asked, eager to shift the attention away from me and Thatcher. I couldn't say exactly why it made me uncomfortable, but maybe it was because things felt so unsettled between us.

Ariel coughed, then pressed a hand to her chest as she swallowed. "He's a good friend. And he's Eric's best friend, so he's around a lot."

Livie jumped in then. "We can't shake the guy. He's so persistent."

Everyone chuckled, and surprisingly, Summer spoke up. "Thatcher is super nice. Nate is too, for that matter. He's not usually my patient. He's one of those people who everyone talks to and seems to get along with—like everyone knows when he walks into a room and is happy about it."

"That's exactly right!" Livie said with a clap.

Katie nodded emphatically, her mouth full of food.

Ariel smiled—small, fond.

Emily finally spoke up.

"I've known Thatcher since his and Bec's days at Fort Campbell. He's a good man, and those two getting together is long overdue. Sounds like I need to meet this Nate Reynolds." She waggled her eyebrows.

Of course her ears would perk up at word of a single man who sounded generally friendly and charismatic. She would need that kind of guy to keep up with her because she was exactly that way—everyone in the room knew her, liked her, and wanted to be around her.

We all chuckled, though again, Ariel's response seemed... small. She wasn't quite shy, just somewhat removed at times. It made me desperate to prod and ask her more, though she clearly preferred a more private approach.

"All right. Enough about these men. Let's talk about the food," Summer suggested, and I loved her for it.

From there, we all shifted focus to the dishes in front of

us, then ended up trotting down a path of favorite restaurants and meals in Europe. Livie and Emily were by far the most well-traveled and had specific recommendations in what seemed like any city someone mentioned. Summer came next. Ariel had been a few places, but mostly listened, and Katie had only been in Germany a few months, so she eagerly took in all the recommendations.

Far too soon, I sat on the train home, rails clacking and car swaying as it sped to my town. Instead of the restless, dissatisfied feelings that had accompanied me on the way there, I rested back against the cushioned seat and felt... peace. Happiness. A hopeful, bright warmth grew in my chest, and it came from the time spent with new and old friends, talking and laughing and building a bond.

The contentment came from friendship and a growing sense of community. And an overwhelming gratefulness for the women—my friends—and the evening we'd shared.

CHAPTER TWENTY

Bec

My grateful heart wore out about six days later. I didn't quite make it a full week before the warm glow of new friendship burned off and I faced another week without Thatcher, the reality that I thought about him constantly, and if I admitted it, a real disappointment in how slowly the days passed during rotations.

The soldiers were all busy, which meant hardly anyone came into the office. Emily had assured me rotations weren't always back-to-back like this—that for some reason they'd scheduled the last six months of this year to be particularly packed. This agreed with what Thatcher had said about the OPFOR soldiers becoming so restless too. *Still.*

Did I want to stay in a place where I only really got to do my job a few weeks per month and the rest of the time I sat around, searching travel websites and spending far too many hours detailing my *places I want to visit* list?

Emily found me aimlessly clicking at some website or another, slumped in my office chair with a murky malaise hanging around my shoulders.

"It's a good thing I'm your friend *and* your boss." She raised one of those brows as she sat across from me.

I sighed dramatically and straightened. "I know. I'm unprofessional, which is gross. I'm sorry."

Her face softened, and the familiar kindness filled it. "There are slow days here—slow weeks. The best part of it is, we do make a difference."

I nodded because I did sense that. Particularly for the OPFOR soldiers, many of whom were much younger than the soldiers on the other Observer-Trainer teams, which were made up of experienced NCOs and officers.

"But..."

I swiveled away from my computer and gave her my full attention.

"If you're going crazy here, I can't tell you it's going to change dramatically. Rotations will slow down in the new year. There's still about one a month until we get into March. We talked about the change of pace compared to your last job, and I'm wondering if maybe you didn't believe me." The corners of her mouth tilted up, but her eyes shined with concern.

"Of course I believed you."

"Maybe you just didn't understand?"

I exhaled. "I didn't realize I don't like slowing down as much as I thought I might. Or I thought I already had, you know? All the time after I arrived in Germany, I did heavy emotional work, so even though life had slowed down compared to how... fraught life at Campbell had been, I was still pretty busy. And, of course, the workdays were busy too. Being here is..."

She pursed her lips to hide a smile.

"Different."

She laughed, loud and bold. "Yeah. Just a bit. It took me a solid six months to adjust to being in Germany *period*, and beyond that, it took another six months to embrace being *here*. I don't want to stay forever, but it has grown on me."

I'd wondered how she'd handled the transition. She'd been my boss at Fort Campbell, and the Ed Center there stayed crazy busy. It partnered with a local university and had a campus building right next door, plus there were far more personnel on post and in the area. It'd been a lateral move for her here. That wasn't uncommon when people wanted to get to European locations. I'd essentially done the same thing coming here to Kugelfels, even though it wasn't an overseas move. Sometimes a transfer to *location of choice* meant sacrificing advancement.

"Maybe it'll grow on me. I haven't even hit my first six months. And there are other things making me feel... off."

Her laugh then came more gently. "Would that be a certain handsome young Captain Wild?"

"Might be."

She nodded because she already knew that. "Do you want to talk it out?"

I breathed in the question, wondering if I did. *Did I?* I'd called Erin a few days ago, told her Thatcher and I were together and I'd made some friends. I still shined with the happy friend glow back then, so I hadn't delved into all the issues. Faced with an opportunity to talk through it, I found I didn't want to talk to anyone other than Thatcher about me and Thatcher.

"No. But I reserve the right to change my mind."

She stood, nodded, and then came around to hug me quickly. "Absolutely you do. And I reserve the right to ask you repeatedly, even if your answer is always the same." She moved to the door.

I hollered after her before she stepped out. "Thanks, Emily. Truly."

We shared a bright smile and one of those looks between friends who really care for each other. Then she left, and I remained, no longer feeling sad and self-pitying, but the longing for Thatcher somehow even stronger than before.

That weekend, I holed up in my apartment and didn't go anywhere. It was a terrible idea, really, but I needed to think. I should've at least hit the grocery store. Instead, I found my state of total inertia oddly therapeutic, so I went with it.

I watched movies, read books, even cleaned, and ordered in dinners. I turned down going to Summer's house for *feast night* and begged her to invite me again. I wanted to be alone with my thoughts—a dumb thing to say, or think, whatever, but I needed the solitude.

Because I'd realized I wasn't sure how long I could stay here. When I moved, I'd planned on several years, yet here at the not-quite-six-month mark, I had doubts. What Emily said about not making big plans for the first six months made sense. It did. That said, I didn't naturally do very well just waiting for some looming unknown. I never had been particularly good at waiting, and after losing Dillon, that ability had shrunk further.

If I left, what did that mean for me and Thatcher? For that matter, if I *stayed*, what would that mean for us?

I had so much *feeling* for him. We'd grown closer while

each holding back. It didn't make sense because I felt so connected to him, desperate for time with him and to see his face and to kiss him, but I didn't feel at ease with him. I wasn't scared, not exactly, but I didn't know what we were doing, or how he felt. He liked me, found me attractive, sure, and yet he didn't seem free and open like he'd been before.

I sighed long and loud to my empty apartment. It wasn't fair of me to expect him to be *free and open* when I wasn't either. Maybe the odd thing now was that I wanted to be that way with him, and felt like I could get to that place. If we just... talked.

And I hoped he could be that way with me too, once we'd discussed the various things we kept hinting at needing to talk about but hadn't actually spoken of.

"That's it. Next time I see him, we're doing it." I said the words aloud to my darkened bedroom, determined to make it so. We needed to talk, and we couldn't keep drawing close physically and having these great surface-level interactions while ignoring the wounds underneath.

Five days until the rotation ended. He'd be exhausted, so I'd plan for him to come Saturday. He could arrive early and we'd talk and talk until we had nothing left, and then we'd be ready for whatever came next.

CHAPTER TWENTY-ONE

Thatcher

I knocked on the door to Lieutenant Colonel Wolfe's office and cracked it when the *"Come in"* resounded a second later.

"Captain Wild, great work this rotation. Really excellent recovery last weekend, too." LTC Wolfe gestured to the empty seat across from his desk, right next to Major Reynolds.

"Impressive stuff, Wild. You're an odd combination of conventional and creative, and it works just right. Keep it up." Reynolds nodded approvingly.

A little flare of pride and happiness for being told I'd done well rose in my chest. "Thank you."

I sat, conscious I hadn't showered in five days and the camo paint on my face had dried and begun flaking under my chin and jaw. They didn't look much better, even if neither had splotchy green, brown, and black smears covering them.

Both Reynolds and Wolfe stayed engaged in the operations out in the box, where we ran our training exercises, as often as they could. I appreciated that they didn't spend their nights curled up next to wives and girlfriends, or whatever Reynolds had, and instead chose to stick it out with the rest of us.

Wolfe sifted through papers strewn on his desk in what I recognized as uncharacteristic disorganization. He and I were the same in that regard—I didn't like clutter.

"You wanted to see me about something?" Maybe I shouldn't have prompted, but the exhaustion hung on my shoulders much like the body armor I'd worn for the last few weeks. Even though it now rested safely tucked in my trunk and ready to go home, I felt the ghost of its weight like a phantom limb after wearing it so much.

"Yes, sorry for the mess here, I'm just—ah, good. So..." He flipped a paper in my direction, then nudged it across the desk. "This is documentation for Project Spartan. Major Reynolds and I have discussed it and believe you are an excellent candidate."

I perked up at this, some of the sleep-deprivation fog receding. "I've heard of it, though I don't recall the details."

Wolfe nodded, and Reynolds spoke next to me. "It's a program that essentially guarantees you a resident ILE slot. While neither of us has any doubts you'd earn one, this is a way to clinch it. Additionally, you get a notifier on your ORB, which makes you look a little special and fancy— more so than you already are, of course."

We shared a congenial chuckle. Sometimes, people ribbed me about doing well, being *special*, which really meant perfect grades in college and being an honor grad in most courses I took. It stemmed from a lifetime of knowing I had to do better, *be* better, in order to prove I'd earned my seat at the table. My parents had sat me down at an early age and explained the realities of being a Black man. Many of them were conversations I'd heard about from friends or even from my sister, Camilla. This one I hadn't seen coming. They'd said I'd have to work harder and be that much better just to be taken seriously. To achieve accolades, I'd need to not only meet but surpass expectations, and when I earned them, I could fully expect to be discounted simply because I was Black and that likely meant I'd been *given* the recognition as a part of a diversity initiative.

At first, I'd thought they were telling me I had to show up and be better because of *them*—both my parents and my older sister were doctors. Yep, all freaking medical doctor geniuses. And by high school, I'd figured out medicine wouldn't work for me. I'd felt pressure like none other once I faced down that reality, though they never made me feel bad about it. Turned out, I had intrinsic motivation and being better drove me—to honor my parents and the way they'd raised me, and to satisfy my own need to achieve. The *be better* talk hadn't hit as hard as it might've if academics and achieving weren't their own draw for me already. With that, though, came the sting and frustration when people brushed off accomplishments for the same reasons they might have discounted me. No way to win, really, but as my family *and* community had taught me, I just kept doing the best I possibly could.

I'd had to ignore the bristling, an annoyed natural response to peers who joked about it, but most did it good-naturedly. Except, of course, those who didn't. I didn't live my life focusing on those moments—worrying about people who chalked up my wins to skin color caused burnout faster than most things. After more than a year with LTC Wolfe and Major Reynolds, I could tell they weren't saying it with anything other than a sense of respect. In the end, what they were proposing showed they respected me, and having these two men's respect meant something to me.

"That sounds good," I said, coming back to the conversation and sensing there might be a caveat.

"It is. Or, it could be. Nothing's guaranteed. There's really no drawback career-wise. It does likely cut your time here by six months to a year, depending on when the board convenes for the program, and when they actually get you back Stateside." LTC Wolfe shifted his focus to the computer to his right and clicked, clicked, then nodded. "Deadline is actually end of November, so we're looking at boards early next year, results by March if we're lucky, and probably a summer move."

My thoughts immediately shot to Bec. I'd have to leave her in little more than six months. I'd be the one leaving her, and nothing about that felt good.

In my darker moments, those selfish, sad, ugly moments I suspected everyone had, I wished she'd come back so I could leave her without a word. Show her what it felt like. I never clung to the idea, especially since the thought of hurting her made me hurt too. Nevertheless, the notion popped up more than once in those first months without her.

Nothing about leaving Bec appealed to me, even if we hadn't worked through everything. The reality of this opportunity couldn't be denied. Ensuring resident ILE, which essentially meant I'd move to Kansas or a few other possible locations and go to school for a year before I promoted to major, would set me up for success moving forward. People achieved resident without that, but naturally, I wanted the opportunity to take a year in person for the course work rather than deal with distance learning.

I pushed away thoughts of Bec. I had no way to know whether this would work out, nor what would happen with her. I couldn't be making career decisions with her in mind. Not yet. "Other than a move sooner, are there other drawbacks?"

LTC Wolfe leaned back in his chair and squinted slightly before responding. "Not really, unless you consider cutting your time here short a drawback. You'll move to Benning and do instruction there for a year—again, assuming they get you boarded and moved in time—and then you'd PCS to Kansas or a sister school for ILE the following summer."

"Sounds pretty good."

Reynolds chuckled. "It *is* good. It puts you right on track with primary zone promotion as well. This is your BZ look, correct?"

"BZ" stood for *below the zone* which meant the promotion board would consider me for early promotion. Super long shot, and I didn't expect it. I'd submit my packet like pretty much everyone did, though most people considered it to be practice for the following year. The main promotion window, known as the *primary zone*, wouldn't pop up until next year.

"Roger, sir."

Reynolds nodded. "Good. Then the only risk is if you get BZ, which wouldn't shock me for you, you'll have to ditch this program because you're an automatic for the resident course."

My heart, already beating a little faster, picked up pace. I genuinely didn't believe I'd get an early promotion, and there could sometimes be drawbacks to that if it did happen.

All that aside, I wouldn't deny the physical response at his positive comments.

"I guess there's no reason not to toss my name in the hat, right?"

Wolfe nodded, a slight smile pulling at one side of his mouth. "That's certainly our assertion. Just wanted to talk to you, make sure you felt good about it and the possibility of leaving early."

"I'm game. Thank you for considering me."

He looked at Reynolds, but I missed the major's response. I gave LTC Wolfe a quizzical look, to which he smiled broadly.

"Thatcher, your performance is excellent. You're someone I count on and whose input makes everyone better. There's no limit to what you'll do in this career."

"Thank you, sir."

"Thank me by continuing on, encouraging your peers, and taking every damn opportunity the Army will give you. You have to go after it, which I suspect you've learned well at this point in your career, but it bears repeating. Make the Army work for you."

Eye contact with LTC Wolfe was intense because he had these crazy blue eyes that just kind of kicked at you. His general command presence didn't push or come out loud, but it definitely *commanded.*

"I'll do my best, sir."

"Then you'll do well."

A few minutes later, I slumped into my car and turned on the engine, hoping it'd warm quickly as the air had that crystalline feeling like it might snow. A bit early for Bavaria, though not unheard of, of course.

As I drove, I thought about who I could share the news with, then talked myself out of that entirely. I didn't actually have any news yet. If the program board chose me, then there'd be something to share. Ben should know. Waverly, Masters, the other officers, a few NCOs... and Bec.

I'd need to tell Bec. And see how it struck her. But there was nothing to tell at this point. First things first—shower, sleep, then go see my girl and figure out how to get past years of hurt, sadness, and distance.

No problem.

CHAPTER TWENTY-TWO

Bec

After going for a jog, cleaning my apartment, grocery shopping, and getting cleaned up, I had ten minutes to spare before Thatcher arrived.

The rotation had ended yesterday, just before I got off work. I wished he'd suggest coming over right away. Instead, we'd made a plan for today during the spotty moments of communication in the last week. He'd been sleeping out in the field for the last few days and was probably super gross and exhausted. I remembered the time when Dillon came home to the apartment we'd shared outside Fort Campbell after a week-long training exercise. He'd been filthy and hungry and tired, and so in need of a shower.

Because of that... because I did remember some things about this side of Army life, I didn't suggest getting together. I didn't want him to reject me, frankly, but I also didn't want him to feel obligated to come over when he really needed to shower, eat, and sleep a good ten or twelve hours.

Had I been able to think of anything else in the last twenty-four hours? No. Had I rehearsed several of the things I wanted to say to him in the mirror? Yes, indeed.

Finally, *finally,* the doorbell buzzed, and I rushed to greet him. I flung the door open to find Thatcher, inevitably more handsome than the last time I saw him. It must've been due to whatever magical man pheromones he had going on that spoke directly to my brain, and it didn't hurt that he held a bouquet of flowers.

"Hi," I said, winded by the sight of him.

"Hey." A small smile, unusually understated for Thatcher, turned his lips up.

And then we just stood there, me at the door, him holding the flowers, not passing over the threshold. I wouldn't quite call it awkwardness, yet it certainly wasn't the joyous, desperate, relieved reunion we'd had days after Barcelona.

Well... we'd never get past it just standing here. "Come in, please."

We moved through his entering the house, me taking his jacket and trying to find a vase, which it turned out I didn't have, so I put the flowers in a pitcher. We hardly spoke, and every second that ticked by caused my heart to beat faster with concern and anxiety over what was coming.

"I have soup and bread for dinner. I hope that's okay. It's a beef stew, so nice and hearty. It's just been so cold, and I thought you might like something warm and cozy tonight after sleeping outside." I gestured to the bowls, a loaf of bread, and the crockpot burbling away with hot soup.

"Sounds perfect. Thank you."

And then, again, we just... stood there. Like we'd hardly

ever met. Like a boulder sat between us and neither one of us knew how to walk around it to get to the other person.

Well, screw this. I'd spent years avoiding my problems and particularly avoiding my feelings about and for this man. At some point, I had to face them, even through this pall of wretched discomfort.

I folded my hands in front of me to give them something to do. "I think maybe we should start by talking, unless you want to eat first?"

He nodded. "That sounds good."

We moved to the living room in silence because that's the way things had gone. I wished more than ever I'd bought one of those little Bluetooth speakers to play music like I'd been telling myself I would so there'd be something in the background.

I sat on the couch, knees pinned together and hands resting atop them like an armchair therapist. He sat perpendicular to me in my cozy chair, also sitting straight and mostly on the edge of the cushion. His large frame swamped the seat in a way that struck me as strangely appealing.

Why would I say that? I'd always loved his height. He stood about as tall as Ben, and several inches taller than Dillon. I loved my brother, but both of us were runts. I liked that Thatcher was tall and broad and even more muscular than when we'd known each other before.

"How was the rotation?" I asked, hoping we could ease into things, or at least move beyond this stilted wreck we'd started with.

"Cold, and it felt long. Overall, a success."

The voice, too. I'd always liked his voice. The last two weeks without him and all these emotions swirling around with nowhere to go, no way to move past this space between us, had left me hungry to catalog everything about him I'd missed. In truth, not just the last two weeks, but for years before.

"Good. I don't know how you guys handle being outside in this cold. Will you have more rotations before the end of the year?"

"Yeah. Two more, actually. The one in December is only a week long and just a few of the teams will have to participate, so it shouldn't make post a ghost town like these bigger ones have lately." He offered a small smile.

"Emily explained how everything worked with the rotations and how it almost felt like the rapture happened when rotations started. I didn't really get it until the last few weeks. I think I kept expecting the next one to be different." I forced a chuckle, remembering the conversation with Emily about how this might not be the best place for me. And it really might not. For now, I needed to focus on this moment and this long overdue discussion.

"Can we—"

"How about—"

We both started and stopped, then laughed in that way people did when they both speak at the same time and it's awkward, but they try to pretend it's funny instead.

"You go," I said, hoping we'd make some headway.

"I don't know where to start. We both know we've got to go back and talk about how we left things." He inhaled slowly, like he needed to steel himself for what came next, then spoke. "You explained you had to leave, and a big part of me understood that. What I haven't ever gotten was why you stayed gone—not just physically, obviously." He swallowed and watched me.

Nerves clogged my throat a moment, my thoughts racing. *This* was the conversation we needed to have, and I had to get it right. I bounced a little where I sat, gearing up to explain without spilling out too much.

"You terrified me, Thatcher. You were so good to me through everything. We were getting close and obviously felt a lot for each other, and then we lost Dillon. And you pivoted right with me to being a supportive friend. You never demanded anything, never made a move, and honestly, I was mad at you about that for a while." I chuckled at the idiotic memory.

He startled. "Really?"

"Yeah. Ridiculous, right? I was so angry about everything. That was just one more thing I could be specifically angry about instead of generally angry at God and war and death, which are pretty futile things to direct my anger toward."

My parents had been an easy target then, too—not that they ever knew it. They kept to themselves after the funeral, just like they always had.

"I'd suggest God can take your anger, but we don't have to argue about that right now," he said, a grin on his lips.

I smiled, remembering that refrain well. The memory brought a measure of comfort, even though the rest of me still shook with adrenaline and nerves. "I'm pretty sure you made that suggestion then, too."

He'd tried to drag me to church with him and Ben—once he'd gotten Ben out of his self-destructive spiral. I'd been processing at home, largely alone, for months before they made it back from deployment and re-entered my world. By that point, I'd already relegated them to surface-level friendships, even though that was ridiculous because we were bonded even more after Dillon's death.

He rubbed a hand across his chin. "I remember."

We exchanged courteous smiles, then I pressed on.

"Everything was covered in this... film. Like a greasy coating that wouldn't come off. The first time I felt hopeful and like I might be able to enjoy life again was when I started looking at jobs overseas. I didn't have patience or words or anything for anyone except for keeping my head above water."

I hoped he could hear the regret in my voice, my words. His face remained calm, and he clearly wanted me to keep going.

"I couldn't see you again. I was too afraid you might have some really good reason to keep me there. I was terrified you might—" My throat forced a swallow. I tried again, my cheeks now burning. "I thought maybe you'd..."

"Declare my love and try to get you to stay?"

The words should've been joking, and his tone almost sounded lighthearted, but it was exactly what I'd feared. And I'd suspected that if he told me he loved me and wanted me to stay, I would've because I'd loved him too. Deep, buried underneath the sadness and anger and pain, I did, and I feared more than anything not having the strength to do what I needed, which at that time was leave. If I'd ever admitted to myself just how much he mattered, how far-reaching my feelings for him were, I would've drowned under the weight of them.

He read it in my non-response and exhaled a sound of true disappointment. "I wouldn't have—that wasn't my plan. The last thing I wanted was to put pressure on you, and the few times we saw each other before you left had been so antagonistic, I wasn't about to wear my heart on my sleeve just for you to grab it and shred it."

He raised a brow, which took a small part of the sting out of his words, though the hurt and resentment were there.

"I'm sorry. I should've trusted you. The thing is, it wasn't *you* who was the problem. It was me."

He nodded and sighed again. "I know. Grief can really mess a person up."

"It can, especially if she refuses to let herself actually grieve." I reached a hand out and he immediately took it, then scooted further to the edge of the chair so his knees jutted out and touched mine.

"You did eventually, though. And I'm glad you did. Ben even told me you'd gotten some help and were doing well over here. He didn't ever say much, but he knew I wanted to know—needed to. That's also when I started really hurting. And honestly, got a little bitter." His brow furrowed, and his beautiful lips, which should definitively always be smiling because nothing and no one should ever do anything to make him sad, tilted down.

"I don't blame you." I studied my hands, wishing for an easier way to plow through this. Wishing that explaining myself wouldn't leave me sliced open. But there wasn't. "For a long time, I convinced myself it wasn't anything specific with you, just a way to move on and have a fresh start. That was obviously a lie since I talked to Erin regularly and even checked in with Ben once a month or so. With you it was just... different."

"Why? How?" He inched closer.

I breathed in, then blew it out audibly. "Because my relationships with them, my feelings for them, had never changed like they had with you. And I didn't know how to function in a friendship with you and have it be this surface-level check-in style thing. I knew it'd hurt us both."

True. But not the whole truth, which stuck on my tongue. I didn't know if I'd be brave enough to get it out tonight.

He released my hand and leaned his elbows on his knees. "It would've."

I nodded. I knew that. And that had been part of the reason. "I also didn't know how to handle what I'd felt for you, how I'd... cared for you, and yet have all the mess I made of leaving between us."

His head dropped between his shoulders and hung for a moment in what I thought was defeat. When he raised it, his expression didn't show pain or regret. A small smile played at his lips and the corners of his eyes.

"We would've muddled through, I like to think."

"Why are you smiling?" I couldn't help the mild sense of alarm that smile gave me, primarily because I didn't understand it.

He laughed lightly. "I'm smiling because you are too stubborn for your own good, and I'm too nice—or honestly, maybe it's cowardice—to call you on it. Or, I have been. I don't think that's going to work if we want to move forward."

"I agree."

He sat straight and grabbed my hand, then stood and moved to sit next to me, nice and close. "I don't want to keep growing closer and yet not close at all. That's what the last few months have felt like to me—small, important steps toward each other, but at the same time this weird distance deep down, still. I don't want to resent our time apart or the way things happened, and on one level, I don't. When we talk like this, I get it, and I see your heart in this and I want it protected. I'm glad you protected it while you were healing."

Speaking of my heart, it clenched, and my whole body warmed. The thought that he wanted my heart safe was just about the sweetest thing, and one more way he proved to be the very best man.

"Do you forgive me? For leaving, and for not calling, and for generally running away from you even though you were only being perfect?"

He frowned. "Not perfect. Don't do that. I was stressed out and worried about you, and I didn't approach things well those last few times we were together. But yes, I do. I forgive you."

I exhaled in relief and said nothing when he tipped his head down like he had more to say.

He continued. "Realistically, I know these feelings have become entrenched, and it may take me a while to break the default pattern they take sometimes. So I need to ask you to be patient with me if it comes up again, which I also pledge to try not to do."

"I need the same from you. I think if we can give each other that—grace and room to forgive when we don't give it —then we might be..." My heart pounded, my body realizing the consequence, the weight of this conversation, and what it might mean.

"We might be... what?"

"We might be really good. Together. For a nice long time." I bit my lip, hope and anticipation fluttering and wild in my chest.

He dipped his head and got close, our faces inches apart, and his arm wrapped around my shoulders. "I agree."

He banished the space between us, and his hand slid to my neck. His delicious lips ghosted across mine, not quite a touch or kiss. "Now what, Bec?"

CHAPTER TWENTY-THREE

Thatcher

F ire. Bec's eyes held fire like she had plans and knew exactly what she wanted to come next. No verbal answer required here. I pressed fully into the kiss and waves of electric heat washed through me.

Being close to her felt like fantasy and need and relief and anticipation tied up into a mass of *thank God, finally.* Her hands bracketed my face and she took. Bec had never been shy about physical interactions. Even our first kiss had been sweet, but *her.* Not that I needed her to lead the way, but damn if I didn't love that she did.

Yet before we could get too tangled up in each other, she pulled back, her cheeks pink and her brow furrowed. "I don't want to push you."

Dear Lord, help me. Her voice had that rich, throaty quality that killed me. "You won't. Let's take it slow, and we'll be fine."

Not that any part of me wanted slow—not at all. I wanted fast, everything all at once. I wanted everything, and I wanted it *now*. But that wasn't me, and it couldn't be us. Not at this point in our relationship.

She must've liked that answer because her smile blazed, and then she pulled me by the collar to her and crushed our mouths together.

"I missed you. This rotation felt long."

She whispered the words into my neck where she kissed a trail while I breathed in the feel of her lips and breath on my skin.

"So long. Way too long," I agreed, my voice low and quiet.

She returned to my lips, and heat coiled in my gut. My hands sifted through her hair and coasted along her back, then urged her closer. Her smooth skin against mine, her fingers running down my chest, all of it long-awaited ecstasy and finally purely pleasurable now that we'd told each other the truth.

Eventually, we broke apart and stayed that way, though neither of us wanted to. Our stomachs had sounded the growling chorus reminding us we hadn't eaten, and taking it slow didn't work very well if you threw all your boundaries out the window and took what your less logical mind wanted.

So she dished up stew while I sliced a loaf of bread, and we sat like people who had their hormones and lizard brains under control and talked. As though our ability to speak freely had been bound up in the web of our past, now we couldn't stop talking—both of us were naturally pretty talkative anyway. We'd had fun on our date and every time we'd been together, though it hadn't felt like this.

Honestly, the last time talking to Bec had felt this easy had been before that deployment to Afghanistan. Before we lost Dillon and everything changed. That thought brought a bittersweet note to the moment. But I cherished the time together because, as I'd long since come to terms with, I liked nothing better than being with her.

"Are you going to tell Ben?" she asked, leaning back against the chair, hands resting at the base of her wine glass still on the table.

"Should I not?"

She smirked. "I'm telling Erin."

I laughed. "Well, then I'm definitely telling Ben. Flint will be texting him before you're off the phone, the old gossip."

LTC Flint was my former battalion XO back in the Rambler Battalion at Campbell, and he'd married Erin, Bec's closest friend. Flint had been with us when we lost Dillon, so he knew Bec and was very close with Ben. And he tolerated me, as I'd made the terrible mistake of going out with Erin on a date *as friends* before they'd gotten together.

She chuckled, then sipped her wine. "Probably true. Then I guess we'll both tell them, and no one will be left out of the loop."

"Good plan."

We smiled at each other, both genuinely pleased. The friends who'd known us during the beginning of our... courtship from afar, we'll call it... would most likely be elated with the news. I always felt like they were rooting for us. I didn't ever speak with Erin, but Ben passed along her good wishes and updates occasionally, and of course, Ben wanted me to be happy.

I left Bec, knowing if I stayed any longer, I'd lose my mind. I didn't want things to go like that, and we'd made plans for the next day anyway. Outside, I hunched against the chill and breathed in the crisp night air. I thought about the evening, and our friends, and the last few years during which Bec had been distinctly absent.

It wasn't like I hadn't been happy. I wasn't the kind to sit down and brood over losses. If a person let it, the past—relationships and history at large—could swallow them. Whether due to my naturally positive outlook, my upbringing, my faith, or all three, I didn't dwell on those things. I had felt that bitterness like a corrosive drip in my heart over the years, and having it all but banished filled me with a sense of newness.

I'd always heard that forgiveness changed the person doing the forgiving more than the person receiving it. I disagreed with that from time to time, particularly when I was younger and I'd been the one to do stupid crap and *needed* forgiveness from someone. Now, forgiving Bec felt like a gift I'd given myself.

I'd told her the resentment might crop up again. And it might, though I hoped not. I prayed as I walked that it wouldn't. I wanted to move on from that, move away from that poison and embrace her apology, believe her, and let the process we'd just gone through cleanse all the nastiness away.

I believed it could, and I couldn't wait to enjoy what came next.

"Hey, man, what's going on?" Ben's cheery voice greeted my call.

"I have some news you might be interested in," I said, the smile in my voice all too obvious.

I'd thought about waiting until the next day, then thought, why? Germany was seven hours ahead of Nashville—no reason to wait when Ben would just now be hitting his mid-afternoon as I got back to the apartment.

"Lay it on me."

"Bec and I are together." *Together.*

Hell. Yes.

"Can't say I'm shocked. I feel like I need some backstory before I can start air high-fiving you and running victory laps around the living room."

I laughed, pure joy at his response and the fact that he could share the moment with me, even from afar.

"We talked. Well, we've been talking. And we've been dating. You know the schedule here puts a dramatic pause on things for weeks at a time. We did Barcelona together for her birthday."

"*Really.*"

Ben knew the significance of the day.

"Yeah, man. You'd told me she'd done the work, and you're right. She's here, living proof of that, and seeing her actually celebrate their birthday... I may have teared up once or twice on that trip, thinking of how happy Dillon would be."

A pause, then he cleared his throat. "He would. That's great news."

"It is. And we had a great time, but we weren't quite through it all, you know? We have this long history and a lot of hurt mixed up in the pain of loss. We'd skirted over a few things when we first got together for lunch months ago. Finally, tonight we sat down and sat down in it. We're in the clear, and now we just see where it goes."

"I'm happy for you, man. Truly."

I smiled at the empty room, though I could hear the reservation in his voice. "But?"

He exhaled slowly. "You know I love Bec."

"Yeah..."

"*But,* I saw you after she left. And you didn't go *scorched earth breakdown* like I did when we got back, but you were a mess for Thatcher Wild, and that's saying something. I know she's done the work, and you're seeing proof of that. She may not realize that being with you brings up other feelings. And I don't want you hurt. Don't get too far ahead of yourself because you guys have a past."

"You know, you've become quite the wise old married man in just a few short years," I said, giving myself a moment to organize my thoughts.

"Yeah, yeah. But seriously."

"I hear you. I do. And you're not wrong. I'm not skipping into this ignorantly. I know she may freak, and I might too for all I know. We talked a little about needing to give each other grace and space to not have the right answers. I think we're on the same page knowing we're moving ahead, happy about it, excited about it, wanting to tell every person we know about it, even while knowing that a handful of conversations is not the end of the story." I picked at a loose thread on the pillow next to me where I sat on my couch.

"Now *you* sound like a wise old married man. You sure you two just got together?" He chuckled, and I joined him. "Seriously, that sounds really... healthy."

"I think so. She learned a lot from therapy, and my parents, sister, and needy friend, Ben, forced me to talk about my feelings."

He laughed flat out at that. "Damn. It's true, I was a needy bastard, wasn't I?"

"No, man. I've never seen it like that."

"I know. Because you're the best."

"Nah."

He chuckled again. "Be modest, that's fine. Listen, I'm happy for you—so happy. And I hope you guys have a great time together, and that one day you call me to say you're proposing, and I get to see what little Thatcher and Bec babies look like."

I shook my head. "You said it."

We hung up, and I chuckled at my friend. A romantic through and through, there'd be no end to his celebrating if we did stay together.

The image of me and Bec together, really together, committed, married with kids... it struck me with a longing that dried out my throat and made my chest ache. I hadn't thought of those things with her in years, though I had to admit they weren't unfamiliar images. We were older, more mature, and it made even more sense now.

We couldn't get there and be apart. And she'd just arrived here. I'd have to talk to her about moving *if* it became an issue. There was no point now, I convinced myself, because it could very well fall through. I hated the thought of telling her about this potentially huge thing and stirring up drama when we'd just gotten over some.

No. I'd wait and enjoy things as they were, and we'd deal with moving and what life looked like going ahead if and when the time came.

CHAPTER TWENTY-FOUR

Bec

I shut the door to my apartment after a jog, and with it, shut out the frigid November air. Good *grief*, it'd gotten cold overnight.

Also, I didn't run all that often these days. I'd run as a coping mechanism years ago, always pushing myself farther and faster, and it'd felt rewarding. The fire in me for it died when I began actually facing my fears. That reality made me terribly sad, too, because Dillon and I had run together. And if there was a place made for jogging, it was the Bavarian countryside. On my three-mile, terrible, painful, awful, no-good first real run in weeks, I ran from my small town to the neighboring one on lovely paved paths that cut through farm fields. It was about the most beautiful thing I'd seen, and I resolved to resume my regular runs in the spring when it warmed up.

For now, I'd need to move things indoors because I had no interest in running in real winter.

As soon as I slowed down after making small laps around my living room to lower my heartrate and try to return feeling to my fingers, a flood of thoughts pressed in. Like always, the run had helped clear my head—one reason the activity had been a fast friend in my early days of grief-evasion.

Thatcher. Thatcher. Thatcher. Thatcher. Even after calling Erin last night, he was all I could think about. Granted, he was eighty-five percent of what we'd talked about too, so that hadn't exactly helped.

Erin had been ecstatic, and of course, insistent I tell her every detail while not actually insisting. I didn't know how she managed that. She was so darn sweet and kind, sometimes I wondered why she'd stayed friends with me so long. That said, I'd supported her through some difficult times too, and we'd bonded enough in person that the miles and years apart hadn't frayed the relationship.

I'd needed girl talk. I loved Emily, but she had a tendency to push me—much like I did her and everyone else. Erin knew my dynamic with Thatcher, or a lot of what it used to be—the strain and frustration and avoidance. Sharing the direct, frank, full conversation from last night had been a way of rewarding myself. It'd been a difficult conversation, but so necessary. Having it behind us, and knowing what lay ahead was up to us... I'd let myself just breathe that in after he left.

Then I'd called Erin. Her new baby squealed in the background, and I wondered at how both she and Ben were parents, or about to be. And honestly, part of me ached for not having that for myself, though not in the way I had in the past. I didn't envy her, and I genuinely loved that Erin had found her home with Reese Flint and was busy making babies and living a wonderful life.

The same for Ben. I loved him like a brother in so many ways, and I wanted his happiness. When he'd called to say Whit was pregnant, I'd genuinely choked up. After their deployment, he'd been hip-deep in grief and Thatcher had a large hand in pulling him out. I didn't have anything to give Ben then, but all along, I'd wanted healing for him. I'd wanted peace. He'd found that with Whit, and it filled my heart to bursting.

These friends' happiness made me begin to hope for my own. The bittersweet pang that had struck last night as the baby sounds had snuck through our conversation reminded me how I'd refused to hope for a future for myself for so long. *So* long. But I'd healed. Not completely, of course. Could one ever heal from such a fundamental loss? I didn't think so. I could say I'd treaded through the soul-scarring sludge of loss, and I'd come out to see the sun.

I'd emerged to find Thatcher again, and though I told my heart to keep itself in check, that things were new and raw and uncertain, picturing that little red-haired sweetie crashing around Erin's living room made me want that for myself.

The want twisted in me and took root deep down, the connection of long-lost primal impetus and hope. I wanted a family and a future, and just like always, I wanted them with Thatcher Wild.

I ignored the unsettled feeling, the discomfort. I silenced the voice that whispered how impossible, how foolish a hope it was. If I let myself think about the unmoving reasons I couldn't be with him and have all those lovely things, I wouldn't be able to relish where we were now.

And I wanted this time, at least for a while. His career wouldn't change—the specter of loss wouldn't change. But I could put that off, just a while longer. No need to listen to that dream-crushing whisper of truth just now.

~

The invitation for Summer's feast came late in the week. I'd accepted eagerly. When I saw the reminder on my phone, I'd messaged her to ask if she had room for one more. Pretty rude, except we were friends, and I'd quickly learned that Summer embraced a *more the merrier* approach to life and would probably be absolutely elated to have Thatcher. When I'd mentioned it'd be him, she'd replied, "Of course, silly! I put you down for two when I invited you."

That warmed me. I liked that she'd thought of us as a couple so automatically. Not that she had any reason not to —she'd seen us in Barcelona, and though she didn't know the full gamut of drama between us, she'd learned quite a bit over our months of new friendship.

Thatcher and I had planned to get together early afternoon. When I remembered the dinner and texted him, we made plans to meet and go to Summer's instead. Someone from work had gotten a running group going and Thatcher hadn't been in a few weeks, so he'd decided to go join and allay his guilt.

I kind of loved that he'd feel bad for not participating. I mean, not that I wanted anyone to experience undue guilt because that mess was unhelpful and downright burdensome. But I loved that he'd feel better joining in and engaging with people, that he wanted to be there when he'd said he would. That was quintessential Thatcher—he did what he said he'd do. It seemed rather basic, and yet few people could really be described that way.

By the time I met him on the sidewalk in front of my apartment, my heart fluttered and my mind went giddy, and I nearly kissed his face off. Except he met my enthusiasm with equal fervor, and the only thing that quelled the connection was a disapproving throat-clearing from a fellow American walking by. Had it been a German, they wouldn't have bothered making a sound. In fact, they very well might've stood and watched, as Americans provided a great people-watching sport for the local nationals, as the military community called them.

"I missed you," he said, a broad smile lighting his gorgeous face.

"It hasn't even been twenty-four hours," I said on a chuckle, pure joy and rainbows and unicorns frolicking through my chest.

"Well, I did."

I leaned up and pecked his lips one last time before we clasped hands and he led me to his car. Not necessary, as it sat half a block down the street, and I recognized the old beat-up silver BMW he'd mentioned purchasing from another soldier when he moved here. Like many soldiers, he'd bought a used car here rather than shipping one from the US. He'd managed to find a reliable one in good shape, though it didn't look great from the outside. He'd lucked out from what I'd seen. Even Livie Anderson-Wolfe had mentioned how her friend Nina had a "beater car" from hell that was a total money suck. I didn't know about all that when I'd moved, so I'd sucked it up and shipped my Prius, and though it cost a lot up front, I'd never regretted it.

Anyway, Thatcher reluctantly released my hand, and the slide of fingers and palms against each other sent little sparkles of delight through my belly. Oh my, how I did enjoy his touch.

The drive only took ten minutes, and when we'd crossed into another little town, Thatcher noted, "I was just here earlier."

"Here as in... Summer's house?"

"No, in Schneiburg. Masters is doing the running group, and we met at his house. He lives here." He flicked his blinker and turned. When he prepared to turn again, he said, "Huh, like... *right* here."

And sure enough, as we turned in, he pointed to his friend's house at one side of a cul de sac. Just two houses down, we easily found Summer's house. Warm light spilled out of windows into the darkening evening, and people gathered around her front door to be let in. Not a huge crowd, though it looked like a decently full house.

"Wow. She's quite the hostess," Thatcher said, grabbing my hand again to walk up the steps.

"Apparently, she does these *feast nights* every other week. She's a total foodie and loves to cook for people. I had to turn her down a few weeks ago, and I have been desperate for her to mention it again, so thanks for agreeing."

He laughed. "I wouldn't say no. I remember Emily saying something about a feast night showing her the face of God, and I've been curious ever since."

We made our way to the door, and Summer hollered, "Just come on in!" So we did, pushing into the bustling home, satisfaction and anticipation at doing so with Thatcher holding my hand pulsing through me with every step.

CHAPTER TWENTY-FIVE

Thatcher

I must've doubled my body weight at Summer's table. At the moment, I sat modestly slumped back against the chair, Bec's fingers laced with mine and her hand resting on my leg.

She had a similar posture—a kind of dazed, over-full, sated bliss. The meal had been one of the finest I'd ever eaten, somehow interesting and new while also being homey and satisfying. Summer truly was a fantastically good cook.

She'd made a Southern-style feast, apparently a pre-Thanksgiving trial of some side dishes she might be featuring at her Friendsgiving, to which I now actively angled for an invite. Instead of turkey, she'd roasted a few garlic chickens—yeah, *a few*. Like she just tossed 'em in there and they came out all golden and perfect and garlicky but not overpowering. Amazing.

The woman herself was scooting one last bite of pecan pie around on her plate, beaming at her guests who all shared the same demeanor Bec and I did.

"That was the single most delicious meal I've ever tasted," Dr. Rashad said.

He worked at the clinic as well—good dude.

"It was... glorious," his wife Jane added, breathless.

"Is there a way I can have a standing reservation for your feast meals?" Bec asked, and everyone chuckled.

Summer's smile deepened. "You're all welcome anytime. Though I do like to rotate so I catch people who don't necessarily have anyone else to feed them."

A flash of... something, crossed her face. I didn't know her well enough to know what.

"That's very kind of you, Summer. We're honored to be included tonight," I said, enjoying the small leap in my chest at speaking for me and Bec.

Her hand squeezed mine, and I looked down in time to see her cast me a look that told me she'd thought the same thing. My chest, like it had on and off all night, warmed again.

"I'm so glad you all came. Feel free to hang out as long as you like. Please know you don't need to stay if you need to get back and prep for your weeks. I know Sunday nights can be tough for get-togethers, so don't be shy if you need to go."

She stood and gathered a few plates from those sitting nearest her. The guestlist tonight seemed varied, though it sounded like it usually was. Several women who were doctors and nurses at the clinic, along with Dr. Rashad and his wife. Sergeant David Reyes and his girlfriend, Nina, who I'd been very happy to meet. And last, a lone man who hadn't spoken much—apparently a German neighbor of Summer's.

What an extremely odd mix. I wondered if she thought through who'd get along best or whether there'd be any awkwardness. Other than the docs, technically I was the highest ranking soldier there. That felt truly odd in the context of a top-heavy post like Kugelfels where so many Majors and LTCs landed. The medical people all mixed well, Nina and Bec chatted education, and David and I knew each other from work. All in all, the conversation had flowed on all sides, and I didn't notice any awkward pauses or sections of the table where the communication broke down.

Bec and I took plates from the others and each carried a stack into the kitchen.

"You don't need to do that, sillies! Get out of here and go spend time together. I've got a great dishwasher—just going to load it up, wipe the counter, and go to bed."

"There's so much to do—we're happy to help." Bec gestured to the kitchen which definitely had more than a few piles of dirty dishes and cooking tools.

"No, no, no. I'm hostess and I get to clean up. You're my guests, and this is part of that. Skeedaddle." She shooed us out of the kitchen with a wave of her hand.

Everyone else began packing up—grabbing jackets and such. Bec and I stood and watched, frankly a bit aghast, until Reyes approached and spoke quietly.

"Seems so rude to just leave, right? I guess it's kind of her thing. She doesn't want people obligated to stay, so she basically kicks us all out. I think everyone here has been at least once before so we know the drill—just pop in and say goodbye, and her neighbor will be the last to leave."

Bec gave me wide eyes, and I tugged her closer with a hand at the small of her back.

"Definitely feels very rude. I think my mother would die." And she would. She insisted on manners and politeness. She loved the conventions in the Army for this reason, though I think she wished I'd married already so I had a wife to share the full range of Army life traditions with.

"Don't stress it. Just say thanks and bye and walk out with us," Reyes said, holding Nina's hand.

Bec and I ducked back in, thanked Summer, and made our way out the front door. Every sense of propriety and rightness hollered at me to go back in there and help finish clearing the table. Out into the chilly night, we chatted with Reyes and Nina for a few minutes before we loaded into the car.

"That was amazing," Bec said, satisfaction still drenching her voice.

"It was. I can't help hoping we get invited for Friendsgiving."

At that, she laughed so loud, it filled the cab of the car.

"What?" I said, wishing I could watch her face as she cackled away.

"You said that so... ardently. And it's perfect because I was just thinking the same thing."

We shared a look, then I whipped my head back to the road, still chuckling and enjoying the lightness of the moment.

This felt good. It felt right that we'd been together with a group—yet we were each other's. It felt good to share in conversation and laugh and eat and toast and make new friends, but hold Bec's hand next to me at the table. All my energy and concentration narrowed to the thin inch where her lips would brush against my skin when she'd whisper something in my ear that she didn't want anyone else to hear. She'd only done it twice, and each time it'd made my breath catch and my blood thrum.

Being with her like this—laughing in the car at both of us being so obsessed with that meal of Summer's—it felt so right to share an experience and come away together.

I reached for her hand and raised it to my mouth. I kissed the chilled back of her knuckles, then released her and cranked up the heat.

"Thanks for inviting me tonight."

She hummed. "Of course. Thanks for going with me."

We settled into silence the last few minutes of the drive, and I didn't say the words that had constantly been on the tip of my tongue, nor did I say something possibly even worse. Things I'd thought before like, *I'd go anywhere with you, all you have to do is ask.*

CHAPTER TWENTY-SIX

Bec

The last few weeks had been perfect.

I swiped through the handful of cheesy selfies on my phone—Thatcher's dark, handsome face next to my lighter and admittedly moony one. I couldn't seem to be normal in pictures lately—when I looked at myself, I swear I could see little hearts in my eyes and adoration in my body language. I wondered if Thatcher saw them too.

We spent every waking, non-working moment we could together. He had some obligations after work a few nights, and I had a girls' night tossed in the mix. Otherwise, we were glued together. Sometimes even the non-waking moments, like the two times he'd fallen asleep next to me on the couch, and I convinced him to stay snuggled up with me rather than venturing out into the cold.

Winter had arrived at Kugelfels, and predictions said it'd be one of the coldest on record. *Goody.* I didn't mind wintry weather, especially when accompanied by snow, but just bitter cold with everything dead? No. Not so much. Plus, my sissy body couldn't run in the cold like this, so anytime I did have a moment to myself, I ended up obsessing over things like how little I enjoyed my job. I couldn't go burn off the angst in the way I preferred.

With the cold came the impending opening of Christmas markets, which I did truly love. And beyond that, there were some nice swaths of time off coming up. Sadly, Thatcher had planned in advance, so we wouldn't be spending Thanksgiving together, nor would we enjoy much time together at all over the Christmas break. His family had arranged to make the trek to Europe, and they would be touring around for a full two weeks. They'd fly into Munich, spend a night at a hotel there, and then they were off on some whirlwind trip through France. Two. Weeks.

And they weren't coming to Kugelfels, so I couldn't even meet them. I'd heard a lot about them, but never actually met them. Honestly, I felt relieved in a lot of ways—I didn't think I could gear up for the excruciating process of meeting parents. I'd done it once before with a college boyfriend and it had been so awkward. Granted, that had been nearly ten years ago now, and to say I'd grown and changed since then was an award-winning understatement. *Still.*

I flipped the phone over on my desk and scooted it away. I had a few reports to finish that I'd been putting off, and I needed to focus for just a few more minutes. A headache settled behind my right eye, and the computer screen made it throb. I inhaled slowly and worked to focus on the task at hand.

Too quickly, I slumped back in my seat. For now, I looked forward to a full five days away from the Ed Center.

The level of boring that'd clubbed me over the head at this point in the month astounded me. Soldiers checked out mentally—they had their eyes on the long weekend for Thanksgiving and then the longer break at Christmas, so few stumbled in to address education issues. Though to be fair, we did have a busy couple weeks after this small break, and it would likely be slammed—or so Donna and Emily claimed.

I'd tried not to bemoan the pace or even the work itself, which after years had suddenly become... trite. Or something. I couldn't tell what exactly I thought about it. I felt distinctly like I'd knee-capped myself by staying in this job and not reaching for something more challenging with this last change. Whenever I got to thinking about that, I quickly reprimanded myself and reminded my whiney mind that I came for several reasons, none of which was seeking a *more* challenging work situation.

Never mind that whole idea bothered me—that I now felt strongly I wanted more of a challenge professionally but, evidently, had no sense of that in myself when making this move.

Enough of all that—I returned my focus to the monitor, squinting slightly as though it would soften the glare of the screen. I made a mental note to order some blue light glasses since apparently my eyes had decided to revolt against the boredom of the job too.

Get your attitude in check, woman.

I rolled my eyes, only to stop halfway when pain jolted through my skull. *Ouch.* I finally surrendered and grabbed my purse, hunting for some meds to take the edge off this pain. I'd hoped to wait it out, knowing it'd dissipate easily enough once I stopped staring at my computer. Probably should've taken a break from screens altogether rather than staring at my phone earlier. Ah, well. Thatcher's handsome face made me do it.

"All ready for your holiday weekend?" Emily asked, wandering in with her extra-large coffee mug in hand.

"So ready." I knocked back the pill with some water.

"You okay? You look a little green."

"Headache." I raised my water and took another large swallow. I'd been neglecting my water, which never helped with such things.

"Ah, bummer. Only two more hours and you can go be free for five days." She wiggled her head back and forth like it held its own little party.

"Yes. I'm so ready. I have no plans, and I'm actually really happy about it."

She frowned. "No plans with the man?"

She knew Thatcher and I were officially together and that things were going well. Since she'd had a few trips for work and had generally been very busy, she didn't have the holiday plan update.

"No. He and a few friends had a trip scheduled for Normandy. All men and all war-focused stuff. It's a beautiful place, though I'll take my Normandy in the spring or summertime, thanks."

She chuckled. "Yeah, I see you struggling with this winter."

"It's no worse than Stuttgart. I'm just a wuss."

"Well, I'm sorry he's gone. I hope you can relax and enjoy the time away. It'll be great to have some time to refresh before we push to the end of the year. We need to get our numbers up."

I nodded agreeably, though my stomach dropped. I hated how dread filled me at the thought of the next few weeks. What'd happened to me? I loved this job. I loved

Emily—she was a great boss. I liked the work and the soldiers and the overall goal of helping people use their benefits to get the education they deserved. Why had my heart filled with such ingratitude for it lately?

I waved when she scuttled out to meet someone asking to speak with her and promised myself I would spend the long holiday weekend thinking about my attitude. It sounded like a punishment, but I needed to figure this out. It made no sense that I couldn't seem to feel anything other than restless while here, counting the hours, watching the minutes sometimes. Even when I had a busy day, I generally returned home feeling like I hadn't done much worthwhile.

Thatcher's presence had helped me avoid many of those musings lately. I could easily put this issue from my mind when he came over or we went out. He consumed me—all my attention focused on him and wrapped around him. Maybe to an unhealthy degree, but it worked out quite well considering it'd allowed me to avoid these ridiculous thoughts. I didn't want to dwell on this lingering job dissatisfaction or anything else negative. I wanted to just be with him and enjoy that. It could be that simple. The warning signs my mind had tried to send me didn't need my attention.

Time to face reality, though. At least regarding work. This weekend. I'd take a good hard look at myself, the job, and attempt to figure out what I wanted. That didn't need to include Thatcher. In fact, it was probably best if it didn't. In the end, I needed to figure out where I was going. Most people didn't stay in the same job, same pay, same position for years at a time—not in their twenties. But I had, making lateral moves to get to Europe. That wasn't unheard of. I needed to be honest—did I really want to continue this way? Did I have ambition for anything beyond this job, this moment? I hadn't been thinking long-term when I moved to Germany initially. I'd only been thinking *escape*.

Now I could admit I wanted more than just escape. That motivation had served its purpose. Now, I felt myself stepping into a new phase, ready to look beyond survival or even healing. I felt ready to think about the future, and what came next... for myself, my job, and maybe even my relationships.

CHAPTER TWENTY-SEVEN

Thatcher

I'd been to Normandy twice before, and it never got old. The military history nerd in me couldn't get over simply being there, soaking up the place, putting clear visions of farmer's fields and beaches into the working historical knowledge of the events.

But I missed Bec to a ridiculous degree. She'd been minimal with text responses, and when I'd called her Friday, she'd sounded terrible—stuffed up and hoarse. Turned out, she was sick. I hated I couldn't care for her. Unfortunately, we wouldn't be driving back until Sunday and since I was traveling with three other guys, I had no choice in the matter.

By the time she opened her door Sunday evening, she looked pretty normal to me. Maybe a bit dark under the eyes like exhaustion pawed at her, and her nose appeared a little red, but overall, still beautiful. Still my Bec.

"I'm sorry I wasn't here for you." I wrapped my arms around her, careful not to hug too hard, not like I wanted to. Now that she was close, she seemed smaller.

"It's okay. Happens."

"How are you feeling now?" I asked, sitting on the couch and patting the seat next to me.

She slumped down and leaned an elbow on the arm, then rested her head in her hand and looked at me. "I'm tired. Doesn't make much sense since I feel like all I've done is sleep the last two days, but I don't feel so awful. I don't know what it was. Thankfully, I haven't had a fever since last night."

My stomach clenched. "You had a fever? I'm so sorry you were that sick."

"It's fine. Burned off the virus or whatever. I don't think you should kiss me, just in case. I wouldn't wish this on anyone." Her dark blue eyes looked sad at the prospect, but still mostly tired.

"Fair enough. I have definitely missed kissing you, but I can wait." I surveyed her place, then returned my gaze to her where she sat, slightly more slumped. "Can I clean up for you, or make you some dinner?"

She rocked her head back and forth in place. "No thanks, I'm good. My cleaning lady comes Tuesday, and I already had some soup."

My mouth twisted to the side to hide a frown. "Okay. Well, do you want to snuggle up for a minute? Maybe watch something?"

"Uh... sure. No TV, though. My head's still hurting."

My heart pinched at her response, unsure. Did this distance between us stem from her being ill? Us being apart? Changed feelings? I swallowed against the idea she'd had second thoughts. She was coming off days of feeling terrible, and I hadn't been there. She wasn't angry, just feeling bad. And maybe I could hold her a while and make her feel comforted, cared for... loved.

My heart sprinted then. Even the simple act of *thinking* the word love sent my pulse racing and a mild vertigo to my head. I gently pulled her to me, leaning back and bringing her to my chest to cradle her close. We both exhaled in relief. Or, my sigh was definitely from relief at having her close again, bringing her comfort, and I imagined hers was too.

In only a few minutes, she pulled away. "I think I might just turn in early."

"Of course. The more sleep the better, I'm sure."

"Yeah. I'm hoping. I haven't called out from work tomorrow, and I'm trying not to."

"Really? You still seem pretty rough."

The look she gave me would've cut glass. "It'll be fine. Plus, I'm saving my leave since I've only been here a few months. It takes a while to accrue after the move."

I studied her face, wondering if I should insist on staying. She wouldn't ask. I'd missed taking care of her, and she clearly didn't feel well still. I could change her sheets or do laundry or clean her kitchen or get groceries.

"Can I go grab you some groceries for the week?" I stroked a finger along the back of her hand.

She looked up, dazed and sleepy. "No. No, I'm just going to sleep."

I nodded, getting the message that any more pushing would be futile, despite the little alarms chiming in the back of my mind. *Something here isn't right. Something's wrong. Stay and figure it out.*

Helpful hints from my anxiety aside, she wanted sleep. I had my own to-do list to get to before work tomorrow. So I hugged her one last time, and against all my better instincts, left her.

The weeks leading up to winter block leave flew by. Unfortunately, I hardly saw Bec, which did nothing to allay my concerns about the dynamic between us when I had seen her after Thanksgiving. We'd done a movie night one weekend and had gone in a big group to two different Christmas markets. All fun, yet there was distance again, and I didn't know why.

Work had slammed her this week—teaching some kind of course and also other stuff she hadn't delineated. I'd gathered her schedule through conversations leading up to the time. I had three days until my parents and sister arrived and we began our big tour of France. Three days until I said goodbye to Bec for a solid two weeks, and I dreaded it.

For now, I had a few items on my list to wrap up before the break, and one of them was another meeting with LTC Wolfe and Major Reynolds.

"Wild, come on in," LTC Wolfe said from his office.

How could he sense I'd arrived? I had no idea. I hadn't stepped fully into the doorway. When I entered the room, Reynolds sat in the seat to my right, chuckling and shaking his head.

"He loves doing that."

"Doing what?" I asked.

"Talking to people while they're still out of sight. I could see by the look on your face you were wondering how he did it."

Reynolds looked ridiculously happy, and when I

glanced at LTC Wolfe, he quickly straightened his features into something serious—but I'd seen the smile.

"Forgive me. I do like to do that. And I won't tell you how."

I chuckled softly. "Fair enough, sir. I suppose command has to come with its own mysterious benefits."

Reynolds laughed loudly at that, as did Wolfe. "True indeed, Wild. Have a seat."

I sat, eager to wrap up this last part of my day and maybe see if Bec wanted me to drop dinner by. LTC Wolfe talked through the updates he'd had about the board for Project Spartan, which were few, and then he got this... look. Only way to describe it.

"We've been tagged with sending a small team to Afghanistan for a quick TDY in January. I'm going to task you with that, and I'd like you to come up with your team."

I nodded. "Thank you, sir. Can you tell me how many I'll need?"

From there, we talked through the mission, which would be an easy advisory trip. I hadn't done one, and of course everyone got a bit spooked by the prospect of these quick trips back to Afghanistan after Sergeant Miller and Captain Waverly were captured last spring. If anything, everyone had been more on guard. They were approaching me this way because no one had been back from the OPFOR battalion since. I appreciated the tact, and if I'd been really disturbed by the whole thing, I probably could've carefully said something and they'd have found someone else. I also recognized that their putting me in charge had significance.

The colonel spoke again, bringing me back to the moment. "Major Reynolds will be going with you, then he'll be breaking off and heading up to headquarters. He'll link up and travel back as well. Get the names to me before you head out on break. Doing anything fun?"

From there, we swapped pleasantries and then I left to make a list before I checked out. I didn't want to think about this trip. I wanted to find Bec, and I wanted to spend as much time with her as I could before I had to leave.

CHAPTER TWENTY-EIGHT

Bec

I'd been weird.

Thatcher hadn't called me on it, like he'd sensed I needed the space to work through whatever this was.

I hated it. Ever since Thanksgiving weekend, I'd realized just how dependent on him I'd already become. I thought about him constantly, wanted to be with him more than anyone else, wanted to see him, touch him, sit in the same room as him... *bad*. Bad, bad, *bad news*. That constant mantra kept swimming around my brain, and I didn't know how to escape it.

So I started pulling back, just a bit. I wanted Thatcher. I also wanted to maintain control of myself. Nothing good came from losing control and falling hair over heels in love with someone, and especially not for me. No.

The only problem with this little plan? It hadn't changed with the wanting, missing, wishing, hoping, falling business. If anything, it ratcheted up the intensity of my pining by about a thousand.

With two days until winter break, and knowing tomorrow would be a quick stop in too, I couldn't bring myself to put him off. He'd messaged earlier that day and said he wanted to come by. I'd avoided him this week due to genuinely being exhausted, but I didn't want to do that anymore. I liked being around him. I liked everything about him.

When I opened the door for him, he seemed tired. The smile on his face turned my insides to mush, and I gripped the back of his uniform just as tightly as he held onto me when we hugged. He looked so good in the uniform too, though I didn't let myself connect the garment to its significance in his life. Thus far, I'd mastered blocking out the true meaning of his work.

"I've missed you. I'm not seeing enough of you, and now we're going to be apart for two weeks." He spoke into my neck where he'd nuzzled his face, his warm breath and chilly nose a stark contrast.

"I know. I'm sorry I've been so beat. I think getting sick kind of took the wind from my sails." No lie. I had felt oddly defeated. I didn't fully understand the feeling, frankly. It was part of the general malaise that'd settled on me at work and another reason to avoid seeing Thatcher, who might ask me about it.

"I'm sorry. Are you still feeling bad? Should you check in at the clinic before the break?" He dipped his head, those brown eyes all concern and love.

I swallowed. I'd seen it before, more than once at this point. And, yes, it hid there. Lurking behind black lashes. *Love.*

My stomach fluttered and my chest clenched. "No, just

tired. Maybe it's the cold too, or just that thing that happens when you know a nice big break is coming and you think about it too much."

We'd migrated to the couch, and he sat, then pulled me down on top of him. I readjusted on his knees, nerves lighting in my belly. I'd only sat on him in heated moments. This was close, intimate, and... nice. Strangely enough, it was nice.

"I want to talk to you."

I chuckled, then pressed my lips together.

"Why is that funny?"

"It's just... you're so serious." My nerves, as though I didn't know this man at all, had taken root, and now I was acting like an idiot. Why was I laughing at him when he clearly had something important to say?

"Well, it is, kind of. It's far too late in coming. I was making sure we could get everything worked out. I want to know if there's any way you could come to France with me."

I blinked. The words slipped into my brain and formed a ball that began bouncing around, smashing my ability to think clearly. "Wh-What?"

"I want you to come to France. If you want to. If you can swing it."

His beautiful face studied mine, a small smile at his full lips.

Nothing coherent came to mind. My heart pounded so loudly in my chest, he had to hear it or feel it. His hand on my lower back must've told him how my body had gone haywire.

"To France with you... and your family?"

He smiled for real then. "Yes. They've heard about you for years, and they'd love to get to know you."

I swallowed, or tried, but my throat had dried out

around his first mention of my going with him and wouldn't work right now. "Oh."

One of his large hands smoothed along my right thigh. "I should've mentioned it sooner. I wanted it to be a surprise, and then... I don't know. I'm sorry I'm just now asking. I really want you to come, and I know my family would love it."

A little puff of air escaped. "I'm working right up until Christmas and then I'm going to Croatia with Summer."

"Ah, dang. I didn't realize you'd booked it." His face, his whole body, sank.

"Sorry. I've been so scatter-brained I didn't realize I hadn't told you. We just locked it in on Monday. Non-refundable." I frowned, both relieved and blazingly disappointed.

Did I want to tour France with his undoubtedly awesome family? Yes and no. Yes because I suspected the family behind Thatcher Wild were excellent people—based on what he'd told me, they certainly were. But did I want to open myself up to even deeper intimacy? Take that huge jump forward? Was I ready for that?

Definite no. Not while I freaked out over liking him too much. Never mind my professional ambition would look like circus peanuts to the Drs. Wild—and yeah, that would be *three* doctors as in mother, father, and older sister.

"Well, I guess you're off the hook then," he said, mouth stretched thin in a regretful smile.

I took his face in my hands. "You're going to have an amazing time with your family, and they'll be so happy to have you all to themselves."

He leaned into one of my hands and inhaled, like he might be drawing strength from my touch. The idea that me touching him brought him pleasure or comfort or strength sent my stomach tumbling.

His rich, deep voice spoke the same thing I was thinking. "I'm going to miss you. So much."

I did miss Thatcher. In fact, I missed Thatcher to the point I nearly felt physically ill. Our quick trip to Croatia lasted only two nights. It was something to get me out of the apartment and eat up a few of the days the Ed Center was closed. Summer had given me a quick exam just to see if maybe I did have a virus or something—I felt ridiculously miserable. It made no sense that my heart hurt like it did.

By the time I got home, having thought of Thatcher approximately one hundred and eighty times per minute—which, yes, did come out to three times per second and made no sense, but deal with it because that was sadly, pathetically accurate—I had to face the truth.

I'd been avoiding it for what felt like months, though it had likely only been since the end of November. My feelings had ballooned out of control, and I couldn't handle them anymore. I couldn't keep them boxed up in a little tin inside my heart, ready to crack open when the time came. Not anymore.

For me, like all of my emotions apparently, this feeling leaked over and out into everything, seeping into every thought, action, breath. I breathed out *I miss Thatcher*, and I breathed in this new truth.

This terrifying, inevitable, life-changing truth.

I loved Thatcher Wild.

CHAPTER TWENTY-NINE

Thatcher

I'd never been so glad to say goodbye to my family.

I loved them, deeply. We had great relationships, got along—genuinely—I missed them when we were apart. That said, bidding them farewell and tucking them into their terminal at Charles de Gaulle airport in Paris meant I was hours from seeing Bec, and that drove me.

The tour of France had been great. The year before, we'd done the UK, and they'd come for spring break after I first arrived and we'd done Slovenia and Croatia. They loved having an excuse to come to Europe, and I loved having them join me. But every minute I was gone, I'd wished Bec had been with me.

What would she have thought of Dijon? Speaking of, did she like the mustard? I had no idea. How had I never asked her that? Did she like lavender? Had she visited the fields when she lived at Stuttgart? Maybe we'd do that together in the spring when the flowers were blooming. Did she like Paris? At more than one point, I'd felt mildly panicked that I wouldn't get a chance to know those things about her. I'd felt strapped down by the obligation to my family and only wanted to run and track her down and shake all the answers out of her.

Or maybe that was the desire to shake truth from her—not about mustard or herbs or cities, but about us. What had happened the last few weeks between us, and had I made everything worse by inviting her to join my family?

I couldn't regret that. I would've gone crazy wondering if she could've joined us, so at least I'd tried. Too late, obviously, but I had.

We'd texted a few times a day, and even called each other on Christmas and New Year's. We'd kept the calls short, which made sense, though it also made my heart ache. I'd fallen completely and irrevocably in love with Bec, *again*, and I couldn't help feeling like she'd started to inch away from me—like she'd laced up her running shoes and set them on the porch.

By the time I'd showered, changed clothes, and made it to her door, the words were on the tip of my tongue. I couldn't hold back anymore. Two weeks of being apart had made staying quiet impossible.

She whipped the door open and sprang at me, clutching me to her before I even got a real look at her. Her arms were around my neck, our bodies pressed close... *thank God*. I breathed out the prayer, truly thankful to be reunited.

"I missed you so much," I said.

"I missed you *too* much." Her voice sounded small.

I walked over the threshold, intent on more closeness. I kicked the door closed behind me and pulled back from the hug just enough to take her face in my hands. "I love you, Bec."

Her eyes flared wide just before our mouths met, a groan of relief and pleasure at the touch of her lips, the slide of her hands back around my neck echoing between us. She didn't run away when I said it, and now the only thing I could think about was this kiss. As always, her mouth met and challenged back, wanting me like I wanted her.

My whole body lit on fire. My hands at her waist and back pulled her closer, pressing her more fully against me. The fizz of anticipation and love and elation at being reunited bubbled through me, and I bent to deepen the kiss. I loved how short she was, but in times like these, I missed those couple inches her high heels usually added. No matter—I squatted a bit, then reached for the backs of her thighs. In moments, her ankles locked behind my back and I held her close.

Having the full weight of her in my arms sobered me. Not because she was particularly heavy. Rather, I returned to the moment—the words I'd just said and how much I wanted to hear the same from her. How much I needed to understand what was happening between us and know she felt the same way—that we were falling together, and she wasn't about to run for the hills.

As much as I wanted more of her, more of this closeness and the thrill of her touch, I wanted the depth of feeling between us first. Before anything else.

A teapot whistled angrily from the stove, providing the perfect break in our kiss, and we startled apart.

"Sorry," she said on a laugh, all breath and a smile.

I shook my head. "Tea sounds good."

I knew this about her—that on weeknights before bed,

or if she couldn't wind down, she had tea. I liked that we'd share her pre-bed tea together.

I helped round up cups and saucers. She poured the piping-hot water over little bags of peppermint, and we settled into seats at the table.

"So, tell me everything," I said, eager for her voice, the details of her life these last few weeks.

"No, you first. How is your family?"

She smiled broadly, and my heart thumped in reply.

I shared a few of the highlights from the trip, then ended with a hint. Nothing cryptic. Just... a hint. "They want to come back at spring break and meet you."

Her answering smile was small, quick. I scrambled to ease her, in case that was too much, too soon, especially in the wake of my confession. "Or, you know, maybe in the summer? No rush, no pressure or anything."

She took a long drink from her tea, and I did too, if only to keep from blabbering on. Then I scrambled to change the subject, to get away from whatever negative feelings my suggestion had caused. I wanted tonight to be full of only good things, good feelings.

"Tell me about your break."

She shared a few anecdotes from Croatia, though not with her usual enthusiasm. In fact, she still had that generally downcast demeanor. Now that I'd gotten over the elation of being in the same room with her, and the adrenaline from confessing my love for her and kissing her senseless ebbed, I saw. She still had darker circles under her eyes, even after vacation and several days off. My heart plummeted.

"Bec, what's going on?" I finally asked after she'd only managed a sentence about how boring her days at work had been before the holiday.

Her lashes fluttered. "What do you mean?"

"You seem... off. I want to ask instead of ignoring it, but I don't want to push." I held out a hand, which she took.

She stared at my fingers, plucking them with hers while she gathered her thoughts.

"I'm pretty unhappy with work. And it's not just Kugelfels. It's more that I've realized how I've been coasting, just kind of settling. I haven't progressed in years—not since I first entered the GS system, really, and that's pathetic."

"Don't say that. You've dealt with a lot, and you moved internationally and—"

"I'm not trying to put myself down. I just... it's true. And for some reason, these last few months have made that click. I feel so disappointed in myself, and I honestly don't know what to do to move forward." She squeezed my hand, and I returned the gesture.

"Have you talked to Emily about this?"

She gave me her eyes—tired, but a little spark of hope there. "Yes, actually. A few times. And she's sending me to a conference later this week—Friday through Monday up at Wiesbaden. It'll be good exposure, and I may be able to network with some people for other positions and stuff."

I swallowed hard. Other positions would mean leaving Kugelfels. I needed to talk to her about my potential changes, though now wasn't the time for that. This was about her, and she was finally opening up, so no way would I redirect to my schedule, ambition, and plans.

"That's exciting. What are the dates?" I pulled out my phone, ready to enter them so I'd remember exactly. I felt scattered after being out of the routine and didn't want to forget.

She hopped up and reached for her planner, which lay

flat on the bar a few feet away. "Looks like the sixth through the ninth. I'll be back late afternoon on the ninth, I think."

My heart sank. "Dang. That's the day I leave."

Her head whipped to me. "Leave? Where to?"

I'd avoided thinking about how to tell her. I'd tricked myself into believing it was no big deal, but sitting here in her living room, I knew I'd been a fool to leave this until now. "I'm doing a TDY."

She blinked back at me, waiting.

"To Afghanistan."

My prayer began before I said the words, and I continued after speaking them. *Please, God, help her be okay. Help her understand.*

That open, curious gaze shuttered at the same time she pulled in a sharp breath. "Afghanistan?"

"Yeah. Just six days. Then I come back, and we start the rotation that next Monday."

She nodded, staring at the planner now. I could see her in profile from where I sat at the table.

"Just six days."

I piped up, confirming enthusiastically. "Yeah, should be quick. Just an advising thing with some NATO and Afghan National forces. It'll be easy."

"To Afghanistan."

Alarm spiraled up my spine. Her voice, remote and quiet, told me all I needed to know about how this news had hit her. "It's low-key. We'll be on KAF, no convoys or anything."

She was still nodding, small, repeated movements. I stood behind her and set my hands gently on her shoulders. She startled, then turned.

My soul shredded when I saw her face. Tears tracked down her cheeks, and she looked shell-shocked.

"I can't."

The whispered words shot daggers at my heart.

"What do you—"

"I cannot do this."

I gripped her upper arms, hoping to steady her, though maybe more for my own sake. "Do what, Bec? I don't—"

Her voice firmed. "I cannot do this again."

I swallowed, my heart beating against my ribs, slamming against the walls of my body, hoping to break out and leap to hers and hold it, calm it, fix all this. "What does that mean?"

She exhaled slowly and blinked me into focus. "I love you, Thatcher."

Her voice broke on the *you*. These words should have sent me taking victory laps around the city. I'd hoped they'd come in their own time, but in this moment, they sounded a death knell.

"You say that like it's a bad thing," I tried, hoping she'd contradict me. Willing her to with ever fiber in me.

"It's not good or bad. What you've just reminded me is that I have been stupid enough to fall for someone in the Army. And even though this weird little training base feels like another world altogether, it's still the Army. And you're going to Afghanistan."

She waited for me to put the pieces together, but I couldn't. I wouldn't.

She stepped back an inch, enough to loosen my grip on her, and wrapped her arms around her waist, cradling herself. "I can't lose anyone else like that. I won't."

Dominoes collapsed against each other in my chest. Knock—knock—knock—knock—until finally my words came. "You won't lose me."

A curt shake of her head. "You can't promise that. We both know it."

My jaw clenched as fury rose up in me. This was not how this night was supposed to go. "I can't. Of course I can't—no more than I can promise you I won't get in a car accident on the way to work tomorrow."

"That's different. Anyone could die that way. That's not the point."

"Isn't it?"

Her chin jutted out, stubborn just like her brother. "It is entirely different. You know it."

"It's six days—not even. This is a part of my life. I can't just turn down every trip to the Middle East. Not very marketable for the career long-term." My voice cut through the room, harsh and ugly with frustration. I crushed my eyes shut and exhaled until she spoke again.

"I would never ask you to do that. That's the point. I've deluded myself into believing that I could—that I would—that you'd...." She growled, anger and exasperation laced through the sound. "I don't know what I thought, but I just... can't."

My throat worked, but nothing happened. I nodded, accepting the momentary defeat. "We're not done here. There's no way."

She pressed her lips together, and her arms tightened around her waist.

"I'll give you space, and we'll talk about this when I'm back. Before the rotation. Tell me you'll make time for me, Bec. I need that, at least."

The unhappy line of her mouth turned down even further, and she dipped her chin. I took that as a promise. We'd talk when I got back. Whatever had just unraveled so completely wasn't irreversible. We could get through this, and I wasn't about to give up without a fight.

CHAPTER THIRTY

Bec

I didn't talk to Thatcher before I left. I couldn't find words to tell him what I needed him to know. I needed him to read my mind and just *know*.

How could he not understand that, to me, all of it came rushing back in that moment? Hearing he was going to Afghanistan, even for six days, had been a sledgehammer to my diaphragm, all air in the room knocked through the window and out of the world. My brother had been killed in Afghanistan. My friend Katie's husband had been captured and tortured not even a year ago, on a similar advising trip.

How could I possibly hear the news that he'd be going there and not *lose. my. mind*?

The reality of his love for me and my subsequent reluctant confession of love for him only made the insanity of our relationship more clear. I'd somehow masterfully ignored the truth of his life in the Army and how fragile I was in its context. I couldn't lose him. I wouldn't survive it. I knew myself, especially now, and I couldn't—wouldn't.

It made me a coward and basically a wretched human being, but I didn't want that risk. I couldn't face it down again, and yet here it was. Whether I liked it or not, he was going.

I did my best to focus on the conference. Met people. Shook a lot of hands and gave out a lot of cards. Did what I went there to do, even if half my mind was elsewhere.

Come Monday, I drove with a singular focus, unwilling to let my mind wander to the reality that Thatcher would be landing at Kandahar Airfield any minute and be in a place I hated without ever seeing. I wanted to be bigger than those feelings, to have compassion for a place that'd been war-torn for literally centuries, but I couldn't. I hated the place. I hated the war. I hated the politicians and people who'd led us there.

That week he was gone moved more slowly than any other stretch of time I'd experienced in memory. The Ed Center was bustling and busy, thank goodness, and yet I had only one thing on my mind. I'd forbidden it to linger on him—on how beautiful he was. How much I loved his hands and his mouth, the angle of his jaw, and the way he shaved his head smooth. I refused to allow my heart to ache in a way that felt like it'd been wrung out, twisted at opposite ends and emptied of everything. I denied myself the memories of us together or that stubborn hope that'd crept in, more and more, when I thought of what might lay ahead for us.

I cordoned off all of these things, and yet, they battered at me, ramming into my consciousness, my chest, and hounding me until I gave in.

He texted me every day at three in the afternoon to say

he was fine and hoped I was doing well, and that he loved me. I always responded that I loved him too. Not to encourage him, but because I'd lived with the final words of a phone conversation and an e-mail to someone I loved, and I wanted to make sure, if the worst and unimaginable happened, the last thing I'd said to Thatcher was that I loved him. Because I did.

Every day at five to three, my heart seized, and I lived in fear I might not hear. And without fail, five minutes later, relief and joy and a sharp stab of pain cut in. Relief and joy because he was okay, and he loved me, and I loved him. Pain because I couldn't do this. Not like this, and not for much longer. What if his next job had him going for six months? Nine? A year again?

No. *No.*

No.

Thatcher knocked on my door at eight the day he got back. He'd been flying for hours and looked exhausted and so, *so* beautiful standing at my door.

Despite the knot of emotion tightening in my gut, I pulled him inside and crushed him to me, relief flooding top to toe, right along with lingering anger, fear, and sadness.

"I missed you," he said, his words a bit muffled since he spoke into my shoulder.

I pulled back and just... looked at him. Took in his forehead, those dark brows and kind, expressive eyes. I couldn't return the thought because saying I'd missed him seemed far too simple. I'd ached for him. I'd shaken for him. *Missing* him was the elementary version of what I'd done, and trying to explain that just wouldn't work.

He studied me like I did him. After the moment stretched thin, his hands slid from my back down my arms to grasp mine, and he ducked his head to look straight into my eyes. "It's over. I'm back safe."

"I see."

His brow furrowed. He'd clearly expected something different—something more.

"I don't know what to say," I said, my voice sullen in my ears.

"I... there's no need to say anything, I guess. It's done. Let's move on. Come sit with me and tell me about the conference. Let me be close to you after missing you, and then we'll do it all again tomorrow." He dropped one of my hands and tugged at the other, leading me to the couch.

Was it all just fun for him?

Didn't he see? I didn't want to keep wishing for him to read my mind or know my heart without saying the words I needed to, but I couldn't pretend we could just go back.

I pulled my hand away, halting his progress too. He exhaled, swiping a hand across his chin.

"I'm sorry. I don't know how to pretend everything is okay." I folded my arms tight across my chest, hugging them to me for support.

"We're not pretending. I'm back. I'm okay."

"This time."

Hurt flashed in his eyes. "Yeah. This time. And I will be next time. I can't promise that, like we said, in the same way you can't promise you won't get in a car crash. We've been over this."

"It's not the same."

He stepped toward me. "Bec, please—"

I flinched away from him and he jerked back, stopping before he touched me. I hated the pained look on his face, the confusion and disappointment, but I needed him there, and me here. I needed him separate from me. He couldn't touch me right now, not again, or I'd shatter.

"I can't, Thatcher. I'm not strong enough."

"That's BS. You're the strongest person I—"

"Person you know. I know. You think that. But I'm not." I swallowed the thickness in my throat. "I'm really not. I'm a coward. Just look at how I ran from you before. Look how I couldn't face losing Dillon for *years*. I'm proud of how far I've come—truly, I am. And relieved and grateful. But I know myself, and I cannot lose you." Emotion choked me, tightening my throat and pinching at my jaw.

"Bec..."

My name came out quiet and solemn, but not a plea. More like an apology.

"I won't survive it. I can't do it again. It's not worth destroying myself over, and I wish I could be brave enough to feel differently, but feelings aren't always rational, as we know. I can't control this fear, and I can't live with it controlling me."

He blinked, my words piling up on his shoulders. He seemed to slump under the weight of them, and the knot of worry and fear and cowardice grew so large in my chest, it threatened to smash my lungs and heart. It must've, since I could hardly breathe, and my heart felt like a hand held it and squeezed.

"I'm sorry," I said, no more than a broken whisper.

He glanced down at his feet and exhaled long and slow. It took longer than I wanted because every second he stayed here was another inch toward the break I felt coming. Finally, he spoke.

"I can't pretend I understand everything you're feeling. Though I can... imagine. I can try. I hate that you lost

Dillon, and I wish I could offer you a version of me that didn't carry that risk. But, Bec, honey, I love you. I want to be with you. There's no scenario where two separate, flawed humans love each other and want to be together that carries no risk."

If I spoke, it'd come out as a sob, so I pressed my lips hard together, working to stay the tide of grief washing over me. I shook my head, hoping that'd suffice.

He shut his eyes against the response, stepped closer, then seemed to remember I hadn't wanted him to touch me, so he held up his hands and looked right at me. "I don't know what to do here. I'm not just walking away, but I don't know how to move past this."

I dropped my head and gave another shake.

"Please."

Tears slipped out of my grasp at the sound of that word, the plea and desperation in it. I hated that I'd caused a sound like that to come from him. I hated that I was hurting him. But the cowering, scared little heart of mine that'd lost too much spoke above all of that. *This is the only way you'll survive it.*

I couldn't lose him, but I could send him away. I'd never forgive myself, and Thatcher probably wouldn't either. Still, it was time.

"I think you should go."

My words came out watery and pathetic. They felt pathetic, so at least that made sense.

"Please, Bec. Don't do this."

Oh, God help me. Fissures split in my stomach and raced through me, my whole body cracking open at that. "I'm sorry. I wish I could. I wish I was stronger. You should go."

I slapped a hand over my mouth to stay the sob that

followed the words, swallowing down the audible evidence of my grief, of the breaking heart now bleeding somewhere in my chest.

He stepped back, then shoved his hands into his pockets while I opened the front door. I had seconds remaining before I lost it completely.

He cleared his throat. "We'll talk after the rotation. We'll talk."

I didn't answer, because what would be the point? He needed to leave. I needed him to leave. And in the end, I'd talk to him again—only to say goodbye. This conversation had clarified what I already knew. I couldn't be here and not be with Thatcher. It'd take a while, but I'd gotten leads at the conference and this made it perfectly clear. It was time to go.

He moved through the door and turned in the hallway.

"I—" He didn't finish. He shook his head, then nodded once, and left.

I shut the door, closed it after the person who loved me and cared for me most in the world without a doubt. The man I was too scared to love back. I slid down to the floor and let myself go, bleeding out the devastation right there on the hardwood.

CHAPTER THIRTY-ONE

Bec

How I dragged myself into work the next morning, on time, I'll never know.

Actually, I did know. I had a mission.

"Are you sure about this?" Emily asked from behind her desk, that single brow arched.

I nodded, steeling myself for the fight. "I'm positive. Obviously, it's not news since we've been talking about it for months now. The conference gave me a new determination."

And breaking up with the man who is undoubtedly the love of my life was a kind of death I wanted to bury and flee.

"I'm glad the conference was so... inspiring."

She studied me, and I did my best to return her gaze, unflinching, though her tone... she knew something was up.

"And this has nothing to do with anything else."

I huffed. "No."

"Really?" She leaned back, arms crossed, that same skewering brow.

Thoughts raced through my mind, and in the end, I wanted her to know. Because as much as I'd sewn myself shut this morning in the cold darkness of the January day, tears sat just behind my eyes, ready to spring out and take over at any moment.

I swallowed, but my throat didn't work, so I took a drink from the water bottle in my hand. "Thatcher and I broke up. It's not the main reason, though it is the reason the time-line has changed."

"Oh, Bec, I'm so sorry."

She reached across the desk, stretching to set a hand on me. I leaned back with a sharp shake of my head.

"No, don't—don't be sympathetic. I can't—I'm barely—"

She waved an arm to erase it all. "Say no more. We'll stay in business mode. I'll get your recommendation written up and sent to the three you mentioned, and you spend the day sending out the applications."

Gratitude flooded my chest, momentarily replacing the wretchedness of the last twenty-four hours—or more accurately, the last week and a half.

I moved through the day with half a brain on work and the other half haloed in a pulsing misery that felt a lot like a migraine. Not a shock considering I'd cried for most of the night, then finally surrendered to sleep two hours before my alarm went off.

The next few days proceeded in much the same way, though the minutes ticking by brought a building tension in my chest, as though the hands of the clock wound a thin rope around me and tightened at the turn of each hour. By the time the rotation officially started, four days after Thatcher had returned home safe and come to me looking for reason and finding only fear and cowardice, I'd graduated to hours at a time without tears and crying.

I spent that first weekend researching the three cities where I'd applied for new jobs—all three entirely new to me, though I'd visited Kaiserslautern, where one of the potentials was. I also cleaned my apartment and packed a bit, ignoring the clanging gongs in my head and rattling in my chest that sounded something like *wrong, wrong, wrong.* If my conscience whispered that this looked a lot like running away again, I silenced the thought. My stupid mind had tricked me into thinking I could be with Thatcher without being paralyzed by fear, without him potentially leaving me in the worst way I didn't have to imagine because I'd lived it. That little voice could take a flying leap.

But by the next weekend, after another full week of the rotation, no news from Thatcher, and generally feeling numbed to the reality that I had lost what I'd wanted so much, time continued to crawl by. By Sunday evening, a knock on my door vaulted my heart into my throat. *Could it be Thatcher?*

I pulled the whistling teakettle from the stove and sprinted to the door, wishing I hadn't decided to give up on the day at seven p.m. and get ready for bed. Instead of Thatcher, I found Katie Miller standing there. "Katie?"

"Sorry to bother you. I got your address from Emily, which she made me swear never to tell anyone."

We shared a smile and a light laugh at that.

"Guess I failed that one, huh?" she said, following me inside.

"It must've been for a good reason. What's up?" I asked, grabbing a water glass and pulling out an extra teacup.

"Uh, well—oh, thanks," she said, accepting the water

and tea I shoved in her hands before nodding to the table as I grabbed my own drink.

"Er, so... you seemed upset. All week. And I just thought maybe you could use a friend."

"That's so nice," I said, truly feeling it. "I didn't realize my mood was that obvious."

I looked down into my steaming tea, but no embarrassment came. I couldn't really be surprised since I'd felt terrible all week, vacillating between angry, disappointed, fearful, and sad. Mostly so heart-crushingly sad.

"Is everything okay?"

Her sweet voice and the general warmth of her... it brought a pang of sadness with it, like everything else seemed to these days. I'd only just started a friendship with her, with Summer, with Livie and Ariel.

"Thatcher and I broke up last weekend."

Broke up was such an inadequate, anticlimactic expression for what it felt like to sever the relationship that was years in the making. To cut away the bond my heart had already knitted to his.

Katie clutched her teacup close. "I'm so sorry. That's awful."

I nodded and eked out a "Yep."

"Do you want to talk about it?"

No, I really didn't. But I did want to know something that only she could answer. "Not especially, but I'll give you the short version. My brother was killed in action six years ago. Thatcher knew him too. We were close before, then drifted apart. We got together a few months ago when we ran into each other—actually, I met with your husband the day I saw him."

I forced a chuckle to break up the sad little narrative. She gave me her full attention, so I kept going, summoning the courage to ask what I needed to ask her, and grateful she'd come to me because I didn't know if I ever would've approached her.

"At the heart of it is my fear. I know that, stark as day. I can't live with it. And I guess I'm wondering how you handle Noah going out and doing what he does after what happened."

"Oh." She set her cup gently in the saucer. "Well... we were in an odd place in our marriage when he was captured. Honestly, we had something of a marriage of convenience."

I blinked rapidly, trying not to look as surprised as I felt because that was so rude. "Wow."

She chuckled, and a genuine, warm smile greeted me when I looked at her. "Yeah. It's a long story. All of that is to say that when they captured him, we barely knew each other. At the same time, and again sparing you the long, weird story, I cared for him and had never been so terrified in all my life."

My throat ached as I swallowed, the mere thought of something like that sending my heart racing. "I can't imagine."

I didn't want to. That was precisely the issue.

"I will never be able to erase the experience of waiting to hear if the team found him, or the flight to Ramstein wondering what shape he was in, or the hours leading up to actually, finally seeing him. I will never be able to forget the memory of him, this big, strong, capable man, lying in bed drowsy from pain medicine." Her voice shook with emotion.

She took a moment, a sip of tea, and I did too. Then she continued, and I braced for whatever she'd say next.

"Honestly, I never thought about whether I was strong enough to be with him. Whether I'd handle it if a similar situation ever happened again. And of course, the odds of that are so, so slim. It *did* happen, and even still, we lose soldiers over there, or in training..."

My heart clenched, the truth of her words stark and cruel and bitter.

"It wasn't the possibility of having to deal with those things again that scared me, in the end. It was the thought of living without him." She exhaled a breath, sighing with a small smile. "I know that sounds melodramatic. Still, after everything, all I could think was how I'd wasted so much time, and how I'd give anything to have a chance to really be with him, for good. Again, it may not make much sense given that you don't know our whole story but—"

"No, it does. I can see what you mean." My heart thumped with recognition. "I hope you'll tell me the story— the full story sometime."

Her kind smile returned. "Of course. But for now, you tell me how I can help."

"Thank you. You already have." My gaze searched around the apartment like it might hold the answers. "I just... I don't think I'm as brave as you."

We shifted gears then, chatting as she finished her tea. She really was a lovely person, and so kind to come here, though I felt my thoughts flatline for anything more than the most basic of small talk. After a while, she stood, so I did too, and followed her to the door.

Before reaching for the doorknob, she turned to face me, clutching her purse over one shoulder and pinning me with a look full of sincerity and concern. "I don't think what you said about not being as brave as me is true at all, Bec. I know we're just getting to know each other, but you're brave. And forgive me if this is too much, too soon, but I can tell you... it's worth it."

She left quietly, like she hadn't come in and slashed all my carefully constructed logic to shreds. I slumped back into my seat and gulped down the last of the lukewarm tea.

Everyone I knew kept insisting I was brave. I had strength. I could do this. Why couldn't I see that in myself?

It wasn't that I thought of myself as a weakling. I knew I'd developed strength and resilience. But the fear—I'd never known anything like it. Not even when Dillon had deployed, and honestly that came down to ignorance and thinking nothing would happen to him. And now? I couldn't bear the thought of losing Thatcher. Yes, I'd effectively lost him by pushing him away, but he was safe. He could go on to live a life and find someone else—

I swallowed down that bitter pill. Because he *would* find someone else. He was far too wonderful and generous and kind—and let's face it, damn sexy—to not find someone new. Someone brave enough to love him.

CHAPTER THIRTY-TWO

Thatcher

My lips were frozen.

Not literally, but very nearly. It was that kind of cold that made it hard to talk because your mouth stopped cooperating, which proved especially inconvenient considering we had a briefing in ten minutes, and it'd be a drive-by at our outside location. Major Reynolds and Lieutenant Colonel Wolfe would be swinging by my company's area before heading to check in with the other clusters of OPFOR soldiers. They didn't often do this. Unfortunately, this rotation had devolved into a cold, frozen mess faster than any I'd experienced. I got the impression it was one for the record books.

"I heard two guys got frostbite on their toes," Specialist Jacobs, the driver for my vehicle, said as he wandered back from chatting with a few fellow soldiers.

"That's awful," I said, saying a prayer for all the men

and women out in this mess tonight, then ducking my face back into the black fleece neck gator I used to shield as much as I could from the chill.

The snow had started a day ago. This kind of snow might even halt business or make for an early call, but when rotations were happening, it wasn't something that could easily stop. Hundreds, sometimes thousands, of soldiers from both US forces and other NATO and cooperating forces—in this case, the UK, Italy, Georgia, and Poland—were mid-step in an operation that'd been on the books for months, if not years. In many cases, equipment like tanks, vehicles, and other necessities, had been shipped via railway months in advance. Snowy weather didn't result in a snow day for us.

Though I could really go for a snow day. A nice cozy blanket shared with—

I shook that thought away. I did not need to be thinking about snuggling up with Bec when we were... whatever we were. She seemed to think we were done. I refused to believe that after everything we'd been through, it was over. I could hear how that sounded—like me, the strong man of the situation knew better than her and her little woman brain. My sister would absolutely slap me for that one.

In truth, during the last few frigid days, I'd come to terms with the facts. Bec might not be able to be with me. No amount of me beating my chest would change that. And did I truly want to be with someone who had to be coaxed into being with me? No. I didn't. I deserved better than that, and I'd say the same to anyone else. So if we hit the impasse of my life as a soldier and her fear of loss again... well, it might be time to work on what it looked like to move on.

I couldn't do anything about it until this rotation finished up, and we still had four more days, assuming we didn't all freeze to death. I needed time to think things through, to talk with her, and to be in a situation where I wasn't constantly exhausted going into these conversations, or about to leave and dive into the next training event or military obligation. We had a few weeks before the next rotation, and I needed those weeks with Bec. If we could make a little progress, then it'd be all systems go. If we got hung up where we had these last few times, I'd have to step away.

For now? I needed my head in the game. Getting distracted, especially in conditions like this, did nothing for me or my soldiers.

"They didn't change their socks," Sergeant Masters grumped from where he sat, still as stone on a small fold-out stool near a burn barrel we'd all used for heat.

Honestly, we weren't particularly covert, but everyone had hunkered down for the night... or until our planned oh four hundred attack. We had five hours to wait, and we couldn't keep the trucks running that long.

"Yeah, bet they didn't," I agreed.

Masters rarely spoke without provocation. When he did, I always listened. And answered, if I could. In this case, he was likely right—you wouldn't necessarily think it, but keeping your socks dry when it was this cold was essential, and that meant changing socks. Those poor guys might've done their best, too.

"Zero-Seven and XO." Masters nodded toward a truck approaching, headlights dark.

That had been one terrifying feature of life here. As the OPFOR, our job was to sneak up and play the bad guys. Because of that, we did most everything under cover of darkness, and that always meant no lights. No headlamps, no headlights, nothing. We used night vision, or NODS, though have you tried to drive in the ancient NODS this unit had? Trust that it wasn't easy.

Jacobs drove me around because, in the OPFOR, we didn't have our own trucks like the Observer-Coach-Trainers, or OCTs, did. They were the ones who taught or coached, and essentially graded, the US and NATO forces on their performance against us—basically they coached them on warfighting, then watched them practice in the rotation, and observed their success or failure so they could, in theory, improve in real-world scenarios in the future.

All of that to say, I didn't have to do the driving, and fortunately for me, Jacobs was excellent. I trusted him, though I didn't relish going anywhere in this weather.

The HMV came to a stop about ten meters from our little camp, and Reynolds and Wolfe exited the vehicle. Normally, they'd be in separate trucks, but apparently, Reynolds' had outright died—no fault of his own—earlier in the day, and they'd had to recover it, leaving him empty-handed since we almost always ran short on trucks.

"Everyone doing all right?" LTC Wolfe asked as he strode into the firelit space.

A chorus of *yes, sirs* and *roger, sirs* passed through the twenty or so men standing around. Most everyone else had hunkered down in trucks or pop-up tents in different locations.

"Good. Proud of you all out here. You get through that zero four hit and then I want you to rotate back and get some hot chow. We've got the DFAC opening for you at zero six. I know it's a hassle to haul in but you can take the morning, get cleaned up, and be back out here after noon, all right?"

Happy exclamations and a few claps and hoots filled the

space. We had all been prepared to camp out a lot longer than that, so this news came as a welcome reprieve for sure.

"Thank you, sir," I said, speaking for the men, though they'd spoken for themselves already.

"You've earned it," Wolfe said, then took a few steps away, so I followed.

Reynolds joined a moment later, and I felt more than saw their eyes on my face.

"We've had four more come in with frostbite. Polish have had a few, as have the Italians. Brits are okay so far, though we're expecting they'll have a few too. We may have to pull the plug on this one early because it's supposed to keep dumping and drop another ten degrees when the snow stops tomorrow." Reynolds clearly took no joy at the news, and LTC Wolfe shook his head.

"Biggest priority now is to execute this last mission and be safe, okay? We're hearing lots of reports about iced out roads and a few places in the back where it'd turned to mud and washed out before freezing, so the trucks are taking dangerous angles. I don't want people panicking, and we tend to downplay this stuff since cold and mud and road issues are no big deal, but I don't want anyone hurt."

"Roger, sir. We'll be on the look-out, and we'll make our maneuvers with plenty of time." Rushing caused trouble every time. I didn't want to sound unconcerned because I wasn't. But we could handle it, and my men were cautious.

"Good. We'll stay a minute to check in with everyone, then we're off to Charlie."

Charlie Company was Waverly and Miller's company, and they had a few young soldiers, plus a staff sergeant who'd showed up to post two weeks ago. This was his first rotation, poor guy. Rude welcome, for sure.

"Thanks for coming by," I said, shuffling back to the

truck to fill in Masters and Jacobs. We'd need to bump back our timeline just a bit so we could move into position in time without rushing. I didn't want to take any chances on the drive there.

And so we did. Hours later, exhausted and freezing, we rumbled at a glacial pace along the tracked roads toward the attack site. And despite the warning from the leadership, our early departure, and extra careful movements, trouble found us.

I saw the truck in front of us flip before I felt that our truck was on the same trajectory, the world inside NODS always just removed enough from reality, similar to a video game. A little like it was someone else hearing Jacobs swearing repeatedly, then the mechanical grind of gears as he wrestled the shift. Someone else's gloved, frozen hands bracing against the ceiling and door, praying everything was in fact secured in the back like it should be so that, as we flipped, nothing would fly off and hit one of us.

Someone else whose helmeted head cracked against the door so hard it shook my ribs, or maybe the ribs shook because of the impact of the vehicle—someone else's HMV, upside down. Someone else's mind fuzzy and face warm and eyes unseeing and thoughts... black.

CHAPTER THIRTY-THREE

Bec

The drive to work had been terrifying.

The post had deemed it a late call just after I arrived at work. This meant everyone would show up two hours later than normal opening times except essential services like the medical clinic and police.

The Education Center opened at seven-thirty, which was a half-hour earlier than most soldiers reported in. Because of this, Emily had warned that sometimes we beat the late call announcement.

So here I sat in an empty building on a largely empty and eerily still military base. I'd always liked that blanketing quality to snow, the way things muted and settled under its weight. But today, it felt ominous. Maybe because I'd given myself forty-five minutes to make the twenty-minute drive, and I'd needed every one of those minutes to travel carefully along the winding roads leading to Kugelfels.

Emily blew through the door, little swirls of snow nipping at her heels—I saw because I stood in my office doorway cradling a cup of coffee to my chest.

"It is *so* cold today." She pulled off a knit cap and shook out little droplets of water.

"I can't believe it's snowing again. I thought it was supposed to be done yesterday."

And though I'd tried not to think of it, I couldn't believe Thatcher was out in it. They all were. It seemed insane for anyone to be out in weather like this, but everyone had assured me they dealt with this all the time and had lots of appropriate equipment.

It didn't help the rocks in my gut that stacked up, each a concern for Thatcher. Was he warm? Was he safe? Could he do his job in these conditions? Did he get enough sleep and food?

Try as I might, the concern for him didn't stop just because I'd broken things off. I now had a job waiting elsewhere and an end date here, which I'd hoped would bring me a measure of peace. I'd assumed that having a definite plan, knowing I was moving and would start fresh again, would free me of this burdensome sense that every choice I made was wrong. So far, it'd only served to increase my anxiety, make me miss Thatcher all the more, and generally walk around confused and irritated. I tried to combat those feelings, but I suspected I had failed after Emily had walked into the breakroom yesterday to find me staring out the window and declared we were going out today—Friday night—and she wouldn't take no for an answer.

On that note, I desperately hoped she'd cancel our plans. I didn't feel like—

The door swung open, interrupting my musings, and revealed... Livie Anderson-Wolfe and Ariel Wolfe.

"Hey, what are you guys—" I broke off before finishing the thought. The matching expressions on their faces spoke loudly. Something had happened. Something was wrong.

"Can we have a seat in your office?" Livie asked, solemn, with a small smile at the corner of her mouth.

"Uh, sure," I said, my voice shaky. Not surprising, considering my heart felt somewhere between completely stopped and already broken. I didn't want to know what came next.

Couldn't be a notification like the one I'd gotten for Dillon. They had to send a soldier of the same rank or higher and a chaplain. They came in uniform, and they didn't come to your work, usually, if they could help it. They—

"Something's happened. They called Thatcher's parents, but we knew you'd want to know."

A sound crawled out of my throat, something like a sob or a moan, and I pressed my lips together.

Ariel reached out and grabbed my hand. "He's alive. He's—his vehicle rolled. Several of them did. Eric and Nate, and really everyone in leadership, have been scrambling since it happened a few hours ago."

A few hours ago. He'd been hurt, and I didn't know. I'd been going about my stupid business, dreading how slowly the hours would pass at work and wondering if he was too cold. Too cold when he was hurt. And thinking about whether the moving company I'd hired would do a good job. If I should pack my Polish Pottery myself, or if I could have them do it... *How stupid.* How inconsequential and just... so.... *pointless.*

"Where is he?" I asked, urgency and fear clutching my lungs and making my breath come up short.

"He and five other soldiers were taken to a hospital in Regensburg. We don't actually know anything more."

"You said it's been hours. No one's there with him?" I turned large eyes to search the room, unseeing. Where was my purse? Where had I set my keys? When had this space become so confusing and big?

"Whoa, hold on. You're not going anywhere," Livie said, a hand on my shoulder.

I whipped around. "I'm going to him. Now."

She nodded. "Of course. But you can't drive like this. Eric just sent me the name of the hospital, and we'll get you there. What do you need to do before you leave work?"

Work. *Work?*

"Nothing. She's fine. Go, and let me know when you get there safely." Emily grabbed my purse, keys, and jacket, and ushered me out of the room behind Ariel and Livie, then spoke again. "I'll take care of things here. Just go."

I wrestled on my coat while walking to the door, then shuffled through two inches of snow to a waiting Audi SUV. I slid into the back and buckled in, and before I could say or do anything, we left.

Even in the SUV, the drive took twice as long as it should've. From Kugelfels, the hospital in Regensburg should've been no more than thirty-five minutes. Instead, we arrived over an hour after leaving post.

Livie and Ariel answered my questions as best they could. They described the rollover—the ice and conditions had made trouble for the soldiers in an unexpected place. They told me how Thatcher and four others had been hurt in the three vehicles that'd rolled, and that one man had been life-flighted but was now reportedly stable.

Unfortunately, no one knew how Thatcher was doing, not even Lieutenant Colonel Wolfe, as the German hospital wasn't forthcoming about details to anyone who wasn't family. After the first few minutes of driving, we lapsed into silence, though my mind was screaming.

All I could hear was *wrong, wrong, wrong*. There it came again, but instead of ignoring it or shoving it down, even pretending I didn't understand, I embraced it. The clanging, rattling, bellowing reality proved inescapable now. I had been so completely wrong.

I'd been scared. So, so scared of the what-ifs. And here I sat, slumped in the back of a car, living a scenario I'd dreaded. Instead of feeling relieved that Thatcher wasn't mine to worry for, I could only think of getting to him. Being with him. Seeing him. I hated that we hadn't been texting, that I might've known something had happened sooner if we'd been in touch—if I hadn't chosen to shut him out.

I had been so utterly wrong, and my idiocy and fearfulness had torn away days and hours and messages and minutes with Thatcher just to protect myself. I didn't want to feel the pain of loss, but *this* was no better. This not knowing, scrambling to get to him, fearing the worst and having no right to the information when the time came...

I thought I'd deluded myself before with the idea I could be with Thatcher and not be terrified of something happening to him. Little did I know the real lie I'd told myself, and that I'd been telling myself for years now, was that I could live a life without him. There was no one else for me, and having him for a short time or a lifetime far outweighed any fear of losing him once he became mine.

He wanted that, and it'd terrified me then, and now, because I wanted it too, desperately.

I'd been so sure pushing him away was the wise choice, like being without him would *ever* be right. When I left Stuttgart, my therapist had implored me to think about Thatcher and why I couldn't bring myself to talk to him. Why I'd run. All through my time with him here since we'd reconnected, I'd convinced myself I was *over* running. I'd done it once and could look back on it with a measure of peace—it wasn't okay to cut Thatcher out so completely, but the flight from Campbell and from him ended with me grieving Dillon and coming to terms with that loss.

What a cruel trick, though. Because while I'd confronted my loss of Dillon, I'd packed away the feelings of loss that accompanied being far from Thatcher, even the thin version of a friendship we had when I'd left. I'd sold myself the lie that we couldn't be together and all my feelings of devastation were tied only and completely to Dillon.

Wrong, wrong, wrong. No escaping it now. Faced with the potential total loss, I had to admit it. My plans to move were me running away. I'd run from reality after Dillon by traveling, then moving, then shutting Thatcher out. And here, I'd run by breaking up with Thatcher and planning to move. I'd used my discontentment at work as a sham reason to justify the change, but at its heart, the same thing that sent me off before would've sent me now.

Fear.

Not again.

The moment Ariel and Livie walked in, the switch had flipped. A cold slap of clarity blustered in behind them and woke me to myself, my plans, and my total folly. I couldn't stand to lose Thatcher, and if I wanted to keep him, I had to try in a way I'd never let myself before. I had to be honest with myself and with him to a brutal degree.

It had always been Thatcher for me, and since we lost Dillon, I'd been running from that truth. My fear of potentially losing someone I loved again dragged me away from the warmth and beauty of the love we had before. Even so, life brought us back together, and this was our chance—my chance—to make it right.

That started now, and there'd be no end to it.

I steeled myself, preparing for battle. I couldn't spend the next few hours or days in a waiting room. I needed to be with him, and I would make that happen, no matter what.

In the hospital, Livie used her considerably better German to find out Thatcher's room. The woman at the desk gave us the information, printed out badges, and a docent led the way. Apparently, we'd just missed the colonel and a few others from the post leadership who were out grabbing food since they'd been there for hours trying to learn something about the soldiers admitted earlier that morning.

"Why are they letting us in right now?" Ariel asked quietly as we walked.

"I told them she's his wife," she said in a low voice.

"Thank you." I'd been prepared to press the issue. Thankfully, now I didn't have to.

The man slowed at a long row of rooms, doors all standing open. He nodded to the first, and I glanced at Livie and Ariel before going in.

My breath caught at the sight of Thatcher in a hospital gown and bed, IV in his arm and a bandage on his head. My heart clenched, a potent swirl of love and fear gripping me.

"Thatcher," I breathed, no tone to it in case he was asleep.

His eyes blinked open.

"Bec?" He struggled to lift his head.

"Oh, honey, no. Stay still. I'm here." Tears pricked my eyes. His voice sounded so tired and worn, and he looked awful. For a man who was composed and capable and gorgeous at nearly all times, it struck me as particularly jarring.

"How are you here?" he asked, his dark eyes shifting between mine and then down over me.

"I came from work. Livie and Ariel came to get me." I stood by the bed and set a hand on his arm, careful to avoid the IV lines.

"Good. Thank you."

I sputtered and choked back a sob then. How could he thank me? After how I'd treated him? We wouldn't deal with that now—not while he was hurt. "How are you feeling?"

"Like I got run over by a truck."

He smiled faintly, and I snorted out an awkward, watery laugh.

"That's not funny."

"No?"

"No."

"I didn't get run over by one in real life, though. Just rolled over in one."

He shut his eyes like something hurt, and I squeezed his wrist gently as though that might help.

I felt useless. "What can I do?"

He shook his head, just barely. "Nothing. Just be here, if you can."

"I can. I am. I'm not leaving until you do."

And I didn't. His injuries were less severe than I'd feared, though he wasn't discharged until nearly eight that night. Livie and Ariel left and then came back to get us, refusing to bring my car since the snow hadn't stopped and they said we needed the four-wheel drive of the SUV, which turned out to be Nate Reynolds'.

I got Thatcher nestled into his house with the help of his boss's wife and sister, which we'd probably laugh about later, and then kissed him goodnight on his cheek. He was drowsy from pain medication and exhaustion, but I heard him whisper, "Don't leave me." I was pretty sure he couldn't possibly have heard my response.

"Never, Thatcher. Never again."

CHAPTER THIRTY-FOUR

Thatcher

Someone had beaten me and left me for dead, then transported me to the bedroom at my apartment.

My eyes blinked open and I took in the familiar dresser, though my wallet and watch weren't where I usually left them. Same comforter as always—navy blue with gray stripes. Same lumpy pillow I kept promising myself I'd replace.

My body was not the same, and as I slowly moved to the side of the bed, I remembered. The rotation. The storm. The ice. The rollover. Waking up seconds after the crash and unbuckling, then calling for a medic and racing around to help Jacobs out. Losing vision in one eye as I pulled him free, then realizing it was because of the head wound gushing. On and on, the memories rushed in until the best part. Bec.

Bec.

I looked for evidence she'd actually been here. Could I possibly have imagined her? She'd certainly seemed like a dream—a stressed out, upset, on-the-verge-of-tears dream, but still a fantasy I wanted to spend time with.

I hobbled to the bathroom, amazed at how sore every part of me felt. I hopped in the shower and washed off the sterile hospital scent and all the days leading up to the accident since we'd been in the field for several days at that point. Poor Bec, if she had been here. I was disgusting.

I wrapped a towel around my waist and eyed the darkening section across my chest where I was already bruising. I didn't bruise easily, nor did bruises show up too vividly, but this looked almost like someone had painted a dark purple slash across my chest like a sash. Lucky me.

"You okay in there?"

Bec's voice through the door startled me, then my heart leapt. I pulled open the door and greeted her concerned face with a large smile. "You're here."

Her lashes fluttered and she swallowed. "You're naked."

"Not quite." I chuckled, then winced at the tight, achy feeling the action caused.

"Oh, I'm sorry. They said you'd be sore for a few days at least." She stepped into the warmth of the still-steamy bathroom.

My pulse kicked. How was this, right here and now, the most intimate situation we'd been in? And with so much distance between us.

She made a sound, then reached up and gently traced the bruise from my right shoulder down to the bottom of my left ribs.

"That looks awful."

Her featherlight touch and proximity had momentarily

stalled my ability to respond. When she looked up in search of my gaze, I cleared my throat. "Isn't it pretty?"

She pursed her lips and a smile hid there. "So pretty."

I wanted to kiss her. I wanted to crush her to me, even if it'd batter my bones. I wanted to shake her, throttle her, for being so stubborn and thick. Maybe mostly the kissing if she kept looking at me like that. But we had too much to discuss, and I was probably about to the end of my ability to stand independently.

"Do you know where the meds are?"

She jumped back. "Oh my goodness, yes. And I'm sorry for not waking you in the night to take them. I actually did try, and kind of got freaked out when I couldn't get you to cooperate, but since you didn't have a concussion, I thought I'd blame it on exhaustion and just hope you were okay this morning. Obviously, I'm an expert nurse. Anyway, uh, I'll grab some pills and you, um..."

Her eyes glazed over as she stared at my waist. I laughed softly, winced at the clang of pain that shot through me again, and met her eyes.

"I'll be out in a minute," I said, not fighting the satisfied smile on my face.

She nodded and pulled the door closed as she stepped out. Pleasure pulsed in my chest—or maybe that was the lingering discomfort from the seatbelt. Either way, I beamed at myself in the mirror. It felt good to see Bec a little flustered by me. I'd felt so damn undone by her for years, and I'd laid it all out for her. She'd rejected it, and me, fearing the risks were too great.

As much as I wanted to sit down in that and take her at her word when she said it wasn't worth the risk—*I wasn't worth the risk*—that wasn't who my parents raised me to be. It wasn't who my God taught me to be. My value was inherent and independent of Bec's love, just like hers existed independent of mine. If she was too scared to take the risk, she had work to do. I'd join her in it, but it wasn't about *me* changing, or even her changing. She had to decide.

And if she couldn't get there, I'd survive it. I'd hate every minute of walking away, but if that was how this had to go, then so be it. I didn't want to leave, and I could handle her needing time to shift her mindset, but I wouldn't hang on and beg for scraps. I couldn't live like that, and I wouldn't.

So if she couldn't see her own value, and mine, and what we could be together, I would respect her and myself by calling it. Though I hoped so hard it hurt that I wouldn't have to.

Not that my assurance and self-worth meant I didn't hurt when I thought about her words, her unwillingness to just... try with me. I'd struggled for days and been only half-focused most of the rotation, wishing I could get back to her and make her see things differently. I'd decided to give it one last shot after the rotation—one last conversation to clarify my perspective, and pray she'd be open.

It was too much to hope that her being here signaled she'd made her decision and it'd gone my way. She loved me —she'd said as much, and she wasn't the kind of woman to say that lightly. If I had to guess, I was probably the only man she'd ever said it to outside of Dillon and her father. Maybe Ben, but it would've been different. I knew I was different for her, just like she was for me.

I pulled on sweats and a loose T-shirt, all the sore... everything... flaring with vivid heat. Definitely time for meds.

In the living room, Bec raced around setting things on

the table—at a place clearly set for me. An omelet sat on a plate with orange juice and water in glasses, and something steaming from a mug which probably meant she'd made coffee.

"Just sit! I have toast coming. You need to eat some real food before you can take these. I hope omelets are okay." She scuttled back into the kitchen.

"This looks great." And it did. We hadn't shared many breakfasts, and never at home, so I'd never had her omelets. I'd never had so many things... *oh, come on, man.*

I rolled my eyes at myself, and even that hurt.

"Here's toast. I didn't see butter in the fridge though." She slid into the seat next to me at the small table—really only a two-person, and I rarely ate here. I ended up on the couch with a plate on my coffee table most nights if I was alone.

"I ran out before rotation. I usually let myself get down to the dregs of everything so I can load up on the way home and feast. I'm sorry I don't have more of a selection."

She'd started slicing into her omelet, then paused, set her fork and knife down, stood up, and leaned over to kiss my cheek. Then, she lifted my chin and placed a light kiss on my lips.

Heat suffused me from head to toe.

"What was that for?" I wouldn't complain. I wanted all her affection and sweet looks. But the gesture filled me with frustration, confusion, and a pulse of anger. How did we go from her sending me away to this?

"You're just so sweet. Who apologizes about the contents of their fridge after being in a near-fatal accident?" She shook her head like I was such a puzzle.

"Not *near-fatal*, that's—"

The cut of her eyes to me silenced my words.

"It could've been. For all of you." She exhaled and picked up her utensils again.

My heart sank low, low in my chest. Here we were again. The risk. Did she think I'd done it on purpose? That I'd asked for something like this to happen just to spite her?

"These things happen. I told you before, I can't guarantee they won't happen again, or worse. But it's not actually that common. I hate that it happened now, right after we—" *fought about it* "—discussed it."

I shoved a bite of omelet into my mouth, chewing aggressively to get food in me. I could feel the frustration, disappointment, and a real sense of upset slithering through me. And at least half of that had to be thanks to not eating much at all in the last thirty-six hours.

Bec took what sounded like a shaky breath. "I'm not saying that. I don't want to get into that. I just mean that you can't pretend this wasn't a big deal. It was. And that guy Bradshaw is going to be out of commission for a while. I don't know how the rest of you aren't in worse shape than you are."

"True. It could've been much worse." I didn't really mean to deny that. With absolute certainty, I believed that truth. The fact that I only had bruising was miraculous. Well, and the cut to my head, which turned out was only about an inch wide, just bled like a fountain. Typical from a head wound, so again, relatively minor.

She reached out and placed her hand on mine. I set the fork down and flipped my hand up so I could hold hers properly and lace our fingers together. My stomach dipped at the contact of our palms and the sweet, gentle look on her face. A half-second later, the swirl of doubt and building anger snuck in again. Though part of me wanted to bury it, I couldn't ignore it anymore.

"I'm so glad you're okay. As soon as they walked in the door, I knew it was you. I don't think I've ever been so scared in my life." She squeezed my hand.

That small gesture, paired with her shaky words, quelled the rising emotions in me.

"Tell me," I said gently, sensing she needed to talk through everything that'd happened. Strangely enough, we hadn't done that yesterday. I'd been given some pretty strong pain meds, so my thoughts had been fuzzy and hard to pin down. She'd been in and out of the room when the doctors came and went, and then a lot of the time I rested and she sat next to me. Having her there had given me so much peace.

The whole time we sat, eating and talking, reviewing the insane events of the last day, my mind knocked against one thought. All I could think was that I hoped, when all this was over, she'd stay. I didn't want her to run again, because I'd come to terms with it. I wouldn't chase her—not if she insisted on running again.

CHAPTER THIRTY-FIVE

Bec

The pills hit not long after we finished breakfast. I needed a shower and a change of clothes, not to mention Thatcher needed groceries and I wanted to be back by lunch. I cleaned up the dishes from breakfast and then kissed his cheek while he dozed on the couch.

His eyes popped open and his gaze found me. "You're leaving?"

The way he said it made my heart squeeze—as though he'd been expecting it all along.

"Yes, but not for long. Just going to shower and change, and grab food. I'll be back before lunchtime." I carefully smoothed my hand over his head, avoiding the small bandage at his forehead.

"Okay."

So many thoughts whirling behind those eyes, and talking through everything now wasn't right. He was exhausted and drowsy from medication, and I... I was exhausted too. I'd had what was arguably the biggest revelation of my life not a day ago; I'd hardly thought of anything else, and yet I hadn't thought about it at all. It'd been there, hanging on the back of my mind like a cape, not exactly helping or impeding anything, but never far from my thoughts.

I kissed his cheek again, breathing in closeness and his warm, familiar scent before pulling away.

"I'll be back."

And two hours later, I returned. I'd planned to give him space, but once I left, the need to clean up, get food, and get back to him drove me through every action. I stumbled through his door using a key I'd swiped from his keyring, grocery bags draped over each shoulder and hanging from each hand, and instantly regretted my clumsy entrance. I shucked my wintry boots and tiptoed into the kitchen.

Upon my entry, Thatcher had sat bolt upright on the couch, then sank a little, like his head had thunked against something when he'd gone vertical.

"I'm so sorry. I didn't mean to scare you." I slipped the refrigerated items into place, then left the rest to deal with later. I grabbed a fresh glass of water and a *butterbreze*—a butter pretzel. The simplicity of a soft pretzel sliced in half with a layer of delicious, golden German butter generously lopped inside had brought me comfort many times, and I hoped it would do the same for him.

"Drink this," I said, sitting next to him.

He took the water and drank the entire thing down in a few gulps.

"Eat some of this," I said, handing him the plate with the pretzel.

He grinned. "How'd you know I like these?"

My belly flipped at that grin and the warmth in his tone. Being next to him after being apart felt right and necessary and consistently exciting, even while he recovered. "I thought everyone liked them."

He turned on a movie and we watched as he ate. I kept telling myself to go put away the groceries, but once he finished his pretzel, he leaned back and put an arm around me. I snuggled in as much as I dared and savored the closeness. I'd pushed him away, and before that, part of me had been gearing up to do so all along. This moment together on his couch with the snow still falling outside felt truly peaceful.

We stayed in that cozy, distracted world all day. And when his touch or scent or warmth or smile threatened to flip the switch on my attention-starved hormones, I slapped the thoughts away. He'd been wincing and grunting whenever he stood, betraying signs his body hurt. By evening, I could tell he was becoming restless.

"Are you going crazy?"

His brow furrowed, then smoothed. He'd gotten used to having to temper his facial expressions because the cut across his forehead pulled and hurt if he became too expressive. Thatcher tended to be pretty animated, so his more subdued approach made me miss the full effect.

"Crazy from what?"

"From sitting around your apartment. You're not exactly a homebody." He liked to be out and do things. He didn't mind sitting at home, and I figured knowing the rotation had continued without him there to help might be bothering him.

"No. I'm worried about everyone, hoping they can get through the last day or so without any more incidents. I'm guessing they're all being super cautious now." His eyes shifted from one of mine to the other. "And—"

I waited, my pulse racing. His cutting himself off sent a bolt of understanding to my chest, and my breathing became shallow with nerves. "Go on."

His lips pressed into a thin, almost regretful smile. "What are you doing here, Bec?"

My heart squeezed inside my chest. "I want to take care of you."

He exhaled sharply, like the words both frustrated and pleased him. "Why?"

"Because I love you."

It might've been thoughtless to shove that out in front and make it the main thing, especially since I'd essentially said *I love you, you're amazing, but you're not worth the risk* not three weeks ago. But my love for him was the driving force here, so there was no other answer I could give.

He leaned his elbows on his knees, and his head dropped low between them. A moment later, he raised it again, his right eye squinting. "It's really annoying how much small stuff like that hurts."

I set a hand on his back and rubbed soothing circles there. "I'm sorry. Only another day or so of it being this bad."

I didn't actually know but needed to reassure him.

He tucked his lips between his teeth and breathed through his nose a few times, staring at the coffee table in front of him. I waited, eager to get this conversation over with and move on.

"I don't want to beg you to talk to me, but I need to understand. I'm getting all kinds of ideas the longer you sit here with me, the more you do for me, and I don't want to be an idiot."

I took his hand and cradled it in mine. "You could never be an idiot."

He chuckled low—not entirely devoid of humor, though certainly not genuine. "I could. I have. And I need to understand now."

I summoned all the courage I'd been working on the last few days, and really, the last few months. What I'd come to terms with—this reality that being with Thatcher was far better than being without him, regardless of the risks—it'd been growing in me since the day I met him. And especially the day I saw him again for the first time. My heart had beaten against its cage in recognition of its partner. It'd taken me far too long to recognize that truth—not just months, but *years*.

"When Livie and Ariel told me you were hurt, my first thought was that I'd been so wrong. *So wrong*. I'd pushed you away to protect myself from what I thought would be unbearable pain, and yet the pain and fear I felt when they said you'd been hurt... it overwhelmed me."

He swallowed, his Adam's apple bobbing in his throat. "Okay."

I smiled at his acceptance of this because he couldn't tell what I meant or where I was going. I continued, hoping I could make things clear for him.

"I realized that being without you the last few weeks and pushing you away wasn't better than being with you and risking losing you. I'd lost you by leaving you once before, and essentially did that again, but the entire time I felt like I was walking against the wind. My whole heart and soul knew I was wrong to push you away. The accident brought that home for me."

"I don't understand."

"I'm not being clear. I... I love you. I always have. And I

want to be with you. This whole thing has made me realize that I would rather be with you and take the risk of losing you, of being hurt, than live without you and feel like half my heart is missing all the time. If I'd rushed like I first wanted to and left for Wiesbaden weeks ago, I don't know how long it would've taken me to get to that same conclusion. But I would've."

He looked ill. "You were leaving?"

I took a deep, deep breath. "I was. After Afghanistan, I expedited my search for a new job. I'd gone to that conference and had some contacts... I cashed in on them and pushed for a near-term start."

My eyes didn't waver from his. I wouldn't hide.

"You never said a thing."

I dipped my head to one side, then the other. "I did tell you how unsatisfied I'd been with the job, and how I felt like I'd settled. The move to Wiesbaden was an impulsive decision, and obviously enough, that changed in an instant."

He stood and moved to the kitchen, the counter creating space between us. Only about three feet apart once I followed after him to the other side of that countertop, but suddenly the words cast us to opposite ends of the earth.

"So you would've left without talking to me. Again."

"No. No, I wouldn't have. I told you I'd talk to you after the rotation, and I planned to." I ducked my head and shook it, then looked back up at him. "I was going to tell you then. They were still getting the details sorted out, so I couldn't have moved before March, probably."

He pushed off the counter and paced a circle around the small dining table. His face flashed with disappointment, sadness, and confusion. "I don't get it. I know we disagreed, but seriously? After everything, you were just going to... split?"

I moved to stand in front of him, but he backed away from my touch. My heart stumbled in my chest.

"I need complete honesty here, Bec. I don't know what we have ahead if we can't tell the truth now."

"I know. And all I can say is yes, my impulse in that panicked, fearful state was to run. Run far and fast and just... change the scene. Then, like I told you, that changed. Drastically. And I won't pretend it happened in the moment of your accident. I think my heart and mind had been at war for a while, and I'd already had several conversations with other people and myself that were leading me to the conclusion I finally and very clearly reached when I heard you were hurt."

He shook his head, then stepped back again just when I stepped forward. My hand darted out and grabbed his arm.

"Please, Thatcher. I know it's messed up. And I'm guessing right now you're wondering what's going to stop me from running again, but—"

"Exactly." He pulled away and folded his arms across his chest. "I don't know how to trust you if I have to worry about you running away when you get scared. Life is scary, Bec, and it's not going to magically change just because you've decided you love me and want to be with me."

"I know. I do know that." I gripped his wrist, still crossed over his chest, with both of my hands. "I'm guessing I'll still feel the urge to run at times since that has been my messed up way of handling things when I first get overwhelmed and scared. But I see the pattern, and you do too. You can help me, and I can work on other coping strategies."

"You sound like Ben."

"I should probably talk to a therapist again. That's where he got all his good material," I joked.

"Not to sound like a jerk, but you probably should. I'm glad you dealt with things when you moved here, and now, it seems like maybe..."

"It's not you sounbing like a jerk. It's true. Therapy's not really a one-and-done thing—going in the past doesn't mean all my crap is over. And the events of the last few months have brought that to my attention. So I have been looking for someone."

I gazed up at him and saw pain and love flickered across his beautiful face.

"I'm proud of you," he blurted, like it couldn't be contained.

I smiled, though my brow furrowed. "Because I'm going to go to therapy again?"

"Because you're brave. Because you're not scared to admit you have work to do. We all do, and it's hard to be open about that. So thank you for being open about it with me." He unfolded his arms and pulled me close.

"You think you can learn to trust me?" I asked, gripping the sides of his shirt. Maybe if I held him in place forcefully enough, he'd know how much I meant these words. This hope.

He ran a hand over my hair, his eyes flickering back and forth between mine. He was quiet for a full inhale and exhale, like he was genuinely searching inside himself to determine whether he could.

"I can. If you can learn not to run away, I can learn to trust that you won't."

"I'm sorry." I rested my chin on his chest and looked straight up at him.

"I forgive you. I'm glad you had your realization before you actually moved, too. I'm glad you're here, and I'm not having to drive to Wiesbaden every weekend."

My smile grew broad and then I laughed. "I guess you weren't going to let me get away with it?"

He shook his head slowly. "I wasn't going to let you get away unless you truly didn't want me. I'd decided I'd have to let you go and make peace with it, but I hoped you'd see how things could be."

My voice shook as I looked in those wide brown eyes and said, with every bit of veracity and feeling in me, "I've always wanted you. I want you now. I want you forever. I'm sorry I couldn't always see or admit that, but there's no going back now."

His chest rose and fell for a moment before he pulled me to him with one arm and crushed me against his chest. My eyes shut at his touch, at the acceptance and relief flooding in with the contact.

"Thank God. *Thank you, God,*" he whispered in my hair.

I squeezed him tight but released him immediately and leaned back, realizing the idiocy of that move on his battered body. "I'm so sorry."

He laughed lightly—genuinely this time. "I'll take it. Even if it hurts, I'll take it."

The smile that beamed out of me felt like a ray of light shining on all the dark, lonely places I'd coddled and protected for so long. "I love you."

His answering smile lit up the room, and he pulled me close again. "I love you, Bec Jones."

His large hand guided my face to his and then he kissed me, claimed me. And, finally, I was ready.

CHAPTER THIRTY-SIX

Thatcher

The six weeks since the accident had been whirlwind. I'd healed more slowly than I would've liked in that I stayed sore and tired for what felt like a solid two weeks. By the time the next rotation rolled around, I was back out there.

And then LTC Wolfe called me into his office to let me know I'd be making the BZ list—I'd be promoting below the zone. All the other nomination stuff for Project Spartan was now a moot point. And I would definitely be moving back to the States come summer.

Pride, excitement, and a thin thread of worry spread through me at the news, at his and Sergeant Major Allen's congrats, and Major Reynolds' cheery encouragement in the parking lot afterward. Good men, and I'd been blessed to have them on my side here.

But that worry hounded me all the way home and

circled my mind until Bec arrived. We'd had dinner together every night I wasn't working except for a handful when she went out with her girls. I'd been borderline nonexistent for my own friends. Waverly had become consumed with the training event coming up in a few weeks, and Masters was helping him train even while he himself still had recovery therapy to attend after being in the accident right behind me and Jacobs.

Bec breezed in, weary from a long day and the bitter cold still clinging to the skies here at the beginning of March. It could very well be another few weeks of winter.

"Hey, you," I said, already annoyed at my weird greeting. I was too nervous, and she'd spot it a mile away.

Sure enough, her eyes cut to me. "What's wrong?"

I couldn't help the laugh that tripped out. "Nothing's wrong, per se. It's just... I have news."

"Oh, nice. I have some too." She set a canvas bag on the counter and pulled out several containers of food.

"You go first, by all means. Also... I thought we were ordering in tonight?" She'd insisted on feeding me for the first few weeks. It was sweet, and honestly a relief because cooking was not on my list of favorite activities, but I didn't want her burdened by it.

"Actually, this is from Summer."

We shared a look. Summer Applegate had also taken on feeding me and everyone else who'd been hurt in the accident as a personal crusade of sorts. She'd sent us all food once a week since the accident. She'd fed five men six different meals, and when she sent a meal, it came *complete* and usually included more than one snack. It was too much. When I tracked her down to thank her and tell her she didn't have to, she made it clear she genuinely loved feeding us. It was hard to argue with that, so Bec and I just made a point to send her thank you notes, and we'd taken her to dinner in Regensburg once.

"What is it tonight?" I couldn't help wondering, despite the more immediately pressing issue.

"I think she said it's bœuf bourguignon with homemade bread. She apologized for not sending salad and dessert." She shook her head in disbelief.

"She's crazy."

"A little. But in the best possible way."

She continued unloading and didn't say anymore, so I pushed, wanting her to share before I did since I suspected my news might cause some friction.

"What was your news?"

She looked up, startled from her work. Man, she was exhausted.

"It's nothing major. I got a few job offers. I was worried turning down the Wiesbaden job last minute after I'd pushed for it so hard might've made me look bad. I mean, it did. But not as bad as I'd feared, when I explained things to them. So I've got options." She swallowed, her eyes flickering to mine and away.

"You want to take any of them?" I asked, not liking the twist in my chest at the thought of her leaving, but knowing her answer might change after I shared my news. Hoping it would.

"I'm not going anywhere," she said, seeming a little preoccupied as she fiddled with the zipper of my uniform top.

She bit her lip and her eyes got that hazy, alluring quality just before we captured each other in a kiss. It was the kind of kiss that would've lit the place on fire, but the resolution I wanted hadn't come. That fell to me because now I was the one to keep secrets, and I couldn't let this conversation end without laying it all out. No time like the present.

I inched her away from me. "I have to tell you something too, and as much as I want to spend quality time with those lips and hands and—everything, I need to tell you."

"Okay, give it to me." She moved to the kitchen and grabbed plates from the cabinets, then began dishing out the still-warm food.

I inhaled and exhaled loudly, then went for it. "I'm getting promoted early."

She froze. "What?"

"I'm promoting to major early."

She set down the spoon she'd used to dish out the beef stew. "Uh, that's a thing?"

I chuckled, letting the action release a little bit of the tension. "Yeah. I mean, it doesn't happen often, but..."

Her eyes brightened and she gave me one of those mischievous smiles that reminded me so much of her brother. "Oh, I see. This is one of those super fancy pants things that never actually happens, but has happened to you because you are so awesome."

I shifted my feet. "It's not all that uncommon. It's a good thing...."

She rushed around and launched herself into my arms. "Congratulations! I'm so proud of you. I mean, it has nothing to do with me, but I'm proud *for* you and of you and I know you're amazing so I'm glad the Army sees that."

Gratitude and love filled me, though I leaned away to get this last bit out. "I'll PCS."

Her face sobered a bit. "Oh.. right. Yeah, of course. Do you know when?"

"June, most likely. I'll start a course that will begin in July."

"Wow. Soon."

I nodded, my chest tight and bracing for more.

"Like, this June, right? In three months?" She fisted my shirt in her hands.

"Yeah. Two and a half. I don't have orders yet, of course. I probably won't for another month or two at least. I'll go to school in Kansas for a year."

She blinked, though she wasn't actually looking at me so much as staring. "Kansas."

"What are you thinking? Please, just tell me."

She refocused on me. "I'm thinking… I could move to Kansas."

My breath caught, and I choked on air and hope. "You could?"

She nodded, but her face looked so serious and her eyes flitted over every part of my face incessantly.

"Would you want to?"

Oh, Lord help me, I couldn't breathe. This had escalated far beyond where I had planned for it to go, and yet there was no going back. This was it. Time to fish or cut bait.

"Would you want me to?"

"Yes. Absolutely. Please. Yes. Yes, Please."

A laugh tumbled out, and she smiled so broadly, I felt it in my chest, my heart thumping in time with the sound and the joy painted all over her.

"Okay then. Kansas it is."

I let out a breath that felt like I'd been holding it since the conversation began. No, since the first time we'd kissed. No—since the first time I saw her last spring. "What are you saying? I mean, I know what I think you're saying, or what I hope you are, or what I want you to—"

"I'm saying you're it for me, Thatcher. I knew it after

five e-mails, and I'm never running from that again. At some point, not yet, we're going to make this thing official, and until then, we're going to keep getting closer and loving each other and supporting one another and figuring out how to pack up our apartments and move across the world together in less than three months... as long as that sounds good to you. I'm not running again. I'm fighting for us, here, there, and everywhere."

I hauled her into my arms and lifted her so we were face to face, then kissed her. Kissed her again. "Count me in."

Nate Reynolds

"Well, we're losing half our experienced officers and NCOs this summer," Eric said from his usual seat, hand threaded in his hair and bleary eyes glaring at the computer in front of him.

"Wild and Waverly are a huge loss, even though it's good for them."

We'd just gotten word that not one, but two of our captains were promoting early. Thatcher Wild, which we'd suspected, and Rob Waverly, who'd had a hell of a year. He'd go on to do great and wonderful things. I looked forward to seeing where both of them ended up.

"Miller's potentially leaving us to head to Bragg. Calabrese is getting snapped up by some special ops unit no one will name. And did you hear Masters is apparently talking retirement?"

He looked personally affronted by this news.

"I hadn't, though I'm surprised to hear Masters is *talking* about anything, especially enough to be caught up in the battalion rumor mill."

The man didn't speak unless spoken to, except on rare occasions. He was completely professional and a very successful soldier, but he just wasn't one of those in your face, loud NCOs. If anything, he was unusually quiet, and I'd seen CSM Allen give him hell for not being direct enough, as though he needed that feedback eighteen or nineteen years into his career. The only time he really went for it audibly was in a fitness capacity, and then Lord help you if you weren't dropping far enough in your push-ups or going fast enough in your run. *Merciless.*

Eric sat up and scrubbed his hands over his face. "He had a meeting with Allen last week. I guess the accident really set him back—he's feeling old and battered. I can't fault him for that, and he's coming up on twenty years right quick."

"I wouldn't place him over... thirty-five."

He made a face. "Really? Why?"

I shrugged. "I don't know. He's not graying at all, is he?"

"He's a blond. How would anyone know?"

"True. I don't know. I guess he must be closer to forty then, like some ancient-of-days elders I know." I gave him a real pretty smile.

He stared at me blankly, not rising to my bait. Then he finally broke and inhaled a burdened breath while clicking through windows on his computer before pushing the mouse away and swiping his CAC card out of the reader.

"I don't want to lose him. I don't know exactly what's going on there, but he should keep at it. No wife, no kids, no crazy exes that I'm aware of... I don't know. I want to make sure he's good from a morale and welfare perspective.

Allen's tracking, and I'm mentioning it to you because I know you torture yourself by participating in his voluntary workouts sometimes, and I'm thinking that might be a good opportunity to just... keep an eye. Check in."

I nodded. "Roger. Makes sense. I'll do it. Consider me the eye."

"Good man." He stood and stretched his neck to one side, then began collecting his planner and mugs.

I took my cue and hauled myself to standing, a feat these days. I was tired. Probably more tired than I should be at thirty-seven.

"You joining us for the hike tomorrow?" he asked as we wandered out of his office and turned to lock the door.

I scratched my neck. "Uh, maybe early? I have a date later."

His eyes cut to me and he gave me one of his big-brother glares that I couldn't read exactly but said something like *why are you such an idiot?*

"Anyone I know?"

"Nope," I said, circling out to grab my stuff as we passed my desk.

"Hmm," he grumped, but said no more.

Yeah. Hmm. Did he want me to hang out with his off-limits-to-me sister? Did he *not* want me to go out on a date with someone he didn't know, like he should be the clearinghouse for my dating life?

No idea. I never could figure out whether he wanted me with Ariel, or just wanted me not with anyone else, or what. Whatever the case, it wasn't his business, and I had to do something to keep the world turning. So... date night.

"Well, good luck, I guess. We're heading out around noon, so don't worry about it if you've got other... stuff. I'm sure Ariel will understand you're busy."

"Yep. Right. Okay. See you Monday."

He tossed up a hand in farewell, and I slumped into my car, potentially imagining the scent of Ariel's perfume lingering there. She'd borrowed my car during the rotation weeks ago, the one when Wild and Masters, to name only two, had been hurt. I'd made a point never to drive with my windows down, and though I suspected it was all in my head, I had no intention of risking losing that.

Pretty much all I had of her these days, anyway.

The end. (For now.)

~

Thank you for reading Bec and Thatcher's story. Keep reading for a link to free BONUS content!

The Soldiers Overseas Romance Series continues with sunny, food-loving Summer Applegate and broody Sergeant Nicholas Masters in The Bright Side of Brooding! Grab your copy today! Or, keep reading for a sneak peak!

ALSO BY CLAIRE CAIN

Veterans of Silver Ridge Series

Small Town Veteran Romance

Love Undercover

Romantic Suspense Light

Back to Silver Ridge Series

Small Town Romance

Exceptional Mission Unit: The Cardinals

Military Romantic Suspense

The Silver Ridge Resort Series

Small Town Romance

Soldiers Overseas Romances

Sweet Military Romance

The Rambler Battalion Series

Sweet Military Romance

Married to the Military Series

Military Marriage of Convenience Romcoms

ACKNOWLEDGMENTS

Thank you to the readers who have been so excited for this book since The Rambler Battalion Series when we first met Bec and Thatcher, and to those who had no knowledge of the characters until they cracked page one. I hope you enjoyed Bec and Thatcher as much as I loved writing them.

Thank you to my A#1, Emma, for being a key voice in this book and providing insights that led to a stronger book, no doubt. Thanks, also, for the beautiful design and the careful details on the spine and back cover—I love the Barcelona city line so much! And for being generally one of my favorites.

Thank you to my Beta readers Caroline, and Amanda! Your feedback helped so much, and I appreciate you taking the time to read through and comment. The in-the-moment reactions are so helpful!

Thank you to jgreads for providing such a thorough, thoughtful sensitivity read. Your insights helped develop Thatcher's final scenes to a much stronger place, and the book is better overall because of it.

Thank you, Jamie, for being my dear friend, sounding board, and writing bestie in this indie life!

Thanks Julie for being my dear friend for decades now, and for understanding me in a way few do. Thank you for loving me and chatting with me and cheering me on and giving me ideas when I'm stuck. You are remarkable, and I am blessed to know you.

Thank you, as ever, to my editor Zee Monodee, for pushing me to do better—to go deeper into the emotions and farther with the perspectives. I love working with you!

Thank you, Amanda Cuff, for wading through and saving my readers from my tendency for passive voice and too-long sentences. I so appreciate your detailed eye.

Thank you to Rainbeau Decker for the gorgeous original cover photo and all the work that went in to making these covers happen—finding real military couples who look like the characters is no easy job, and you've made my vision real!

Thanks to Matthew and the kids for being so supportive. I say it every book, but it never changes—your genuine support of my writing is one of so many ways you love me well. Thank you. Thanks also to my mom who reads every book and gives me feedback and finds the typos no one else dares mention to me. I love you!

ABOUT THE AUTHOR

Claire Cain lives to eat and drink her way around the globe with her traveling soldier and three kids, but is perhaps even happier hunkered down at home in a pair of sweatpants and slippers using any free moment she has to read and cook. Or talk—she really likes to talk. She has become an expert at packing too many dishes in too few cabinets and making houses into homes from Utah to Germany and many places in between. She's a proud Army wife and is frankly just really happy to be here.

You can also join Claire's facebook reader group for exclusive content and fun: https://www.facebook.com/groups/clairecain/

Website: http://www.clairecainwriter.com

E-mail: Claire@ClaireCainWriter.com

Newsletter sign-up for new releases, exclusives, and freebies: http://www.clairecainwriter.com/newsletter

SNEAK PEEK - THE BRIGHT SIDE OF BROODING

Check out a sneak peek of The Bright Side of Brooding. I think you're going to love Nick and Summer. Enjoy this snippet, and get it today!

Summer

Angry wouldn't quite describe his face. But suspicious? Yes.

He cut an imposing figure, I had to admit. He embodied that large, intimidating, mean-mugging type man I typically didn't go for. But every time I encountered Nicholas Masters, whether in life or legend, some element revealed itself that caught me off guard and forced me to notice him.

For example? That letter. Who writes a letter like that? Or when Rob mentioned he lives just a few doors down from my house. This came in the context of him sharing Masters' address when I explained wanting to make food for the people who'd been in the accident. After Rob gave it, he told me not to share it, not to tell anyone I was feeding

Masters in the first place, and that the only reason he knew where Masters lived was because he sometimes trained at his house.

What?

I knew Rob was training for something, and it occupied most of his time outside the workday. But to find it was Nicholas Masters who was training him? It... intrigued me.

Even the time at the fest, when he'd just left. More than a small handful of women had approached him in the hour he'd sat at the table. I'd missed his dismissal of them, but it'd happened, and quickly. This, too, served to intrigue me.

But nothing could've prepared me for the sight in front of me. Because it was—and please don't think less of me for saying so—something right out of a pinup calendar. Whatever the case, I would just be thankful for the moment, even if it came with the storm cloud of his facial expression.

The man stood in his doorway, warm light behind him lending him an unearthly, angelic glow. His feet were bare on the hardwood floor just inside the threshold, and his long, muscular legs were covered in sweatpants pushed up at his calves. And up top?

Nothing. Not. A. Thing. Just miles of stunning golden skin interrupted by designs inking over every part of his arms. Well, skin and ink that covered muscles carved out of will and sacrifice. Muscles defined by refusing bread and cheese and butter, no doubt.

And yes—yes, that would be a sight in and of itself. But in one arm, cradled like a baby, rested a little white ball of fur with cerulean blue eyes blinking back at me and a long tail flicking with impatience.

He was topless. With a kitten. In a snowstorm.

Seriously.

Read Nick and Summer's story today!